Billion-Dollar Bachelors

Business isn't the only thing making their heads spin!

Meet three billionaire friends—Ted Fincher, Sawyer Mahoney and Ronan Gerard—who channeled their brains, brawn and ambition to start the mega-successful Big Think Corp. Their aim is to save the world, one project at a time!

But while they have success in business, their love lives need work! When Ted is interviewed by effervescent journalist Adelaid, things turn passionate, and they have a shocking surprise in store.

Sawyer attends the birthday party of his best friend's sister, and when reunited with Petra, feelings they thought they had buried long ago come crashing to the surface...

Ronan is very protective of receptionist Gia. But after she resigns, they begin to disentangle the ties that have bound them this far, to find that they've been entangled in a whole other way all along!

Find out what happens in Ted's story in
Whirlwind Fling to Baby Bombshell
Available now!

And look out for Sawyer and Petra's story
Fake Engagement with the Billionaire
and
Ronan and Gia's story
Cinderella Assistant to Boss's Bride

Coming in 2023 from Harlequin Romance!

Dear Reader,

Welcome to the Billion-Dollar Bachelors series! I'm so excited for you to get your first glimpse of Ted, Sawyer and Ronan; respectively the brains, brawn and brass behind Big Think Corp.

The Big Think boys have big reputations and big personalities to match. So, finding the right heroines to match with them has been great fun.

Which brings us to Adelaid Adams. I'm not sure I've ever written a heroine as close to my heart as Adelaid. From her moniker to her love of stationery and old movies; her dreamy, distractable mind; and her passion for breeding empathy through words, there is a lot of me in her. So naturally, I hope you love her as much as I do!

As for Ted—a six-foot-five genius cinnamon roll with crooked glasses, great purpose and a knight-in-shining-armor complex—I have zero doubt you'll all fall madly in love with him.

Add Melbourne, the city of my heart, and a smattering of fun, warm, whimsical secondary characters—some of whom might just show up in future Billion-Dollar Bachelors books ;)—I am thrilled to offer up to you my latest story, *Whirlwind Fling to Baby Bombshell*.

Happy reading!

Love,

Ally

Whirlwind Fling to Baby Bombshell

Ally Blake

Recycling programs
for this product may
not exist in your area.

ISBN-13: 978-1-335-73687-1

Whirlwind Fling to Baby Bombshell

Copyright © 2022 by Ally Blake

For questions and comments about the quality of this book,
please contact us at CustomerService@Harlequin.com.

Harlequin Enterprises ULC
22 Adelaide St. West, 41st Floor
Toronto, Ontario M5H 4E3, Canada
www.Harlequin.com

Printed in U.S.A.

Australian author **Ally Blake** loves reading and strong coffee, porch swings and dappled sunshine, beautiful notebooks and soft, dark pencils. Her inquisitive, rambunctious, spectacular children are her exquisite delights. And she adores writing love stories so much she'd write them even if nobody else read them. No wonder, then, having sold over four million copies of her romance novels worldwide, Ally is living her bliss. Find out more about Ally's books at allyblake.com.

Books by Ally Blake

Harlequin Romance

A Fairytale Summer!

Dream Vacation, Surprise Baby

The Royals of Vallemont

Rescuing the Royal Runaway Bride
Amber and the Rogue Prince

Hired by the Mysterious Millionaire
A Week with the Best Man
Crazy About Her Impossible Boss
Brooding Rebel to Baby Daddy
The Millionaire's Melbourne Proposal
The Wedding Favor

Harlequin KISS

The Dance Off
Her Hottest Summer Yet

Visit the Author Profile page
at Harlequin.com for more titles.

To libraries and the librarians within them. For the books recommended, the hot desks away from home, the heartwarming support of my writing and the ever-constant sanctuary—thank you from the bottom of my adoring heart.

Praise for
Ally Blake

"I found *Hired by the Mysterious Millionaire* by Ally Blake to be a fascinating read... The story of how they get to their HEA is a page-turner. 'Love conquers all' and does so in a very entertaining way in this book."

—*Harlequin Junkie*

CHAPTER ONE

A COLE PORTER PLAYLIST crooning through her earbuds, hand shielding her face from the brilliance of Melbourne's sharp autumnal sun, Adelaid Adams took in the sublime façade of the Big Think Corp building, a sense of inevitability quickening inside of her.

For once she stopped faffing about outside and walked through those doors, she would be taking a genuine step towards her dream career.

And yet, her feet did not move.

Adelaid tugged on the cuff of her houndstooth jacket, the chafe of vintage wool over her fingertips helping her stay inside her own skin. With its sharp shoulder pads and wide-legged pants, the moment she'd seen the op shop suit she'd thought, *Katharine Hepburn!* Woman of the Year!

"Dress for the life you want, not the life you have," Adelaid's mother used to say, while swanning around the kitchen wearing a feather-lined satin robe, martini in hand at eight in the morning on a school day. As if the life *she'd* wanted

was one of a once-lauded nineteen-forties movie star on the downhill slide.

Adelaid had definitely inherited the grandiosity of her mother's dreams, among other things, though hers were hopefully more achievable. Along the lines of "highly respected, sartorially envied writer of warm, witty, winning profiles that stun readers with their erudite observations, empathy and heart."

But a girl had to eat, so she'd kept the cushy digital media job she'd taken on right out of uni. Writing lists such as *Top Ten Mafia Reverse Harem Christmas Novels* and creating cutesy "click-happy" headlines for a wonderful editor who trusted her to do her thing and penning stories of quiet heroism for community publications, for little money, on the side.

Till last week, that was. When she'd given it all away. For the chance to walk through the gigantic rotating glass doors, and interview one Ted Fincher.

Ted Fincher one of the trio of hotshot, wunderkind, zillionaire founders behind the inventive, innovative, future-focussed juggernaut that was Big Think Corp.

World-renowned scientist lousy with international prizes, scientific breakthroughs galore and more qualifications than she had shoes was rather a step up from telling tales of retired nurses, or dogs that saved their owners' lives.

But people were people. And she was ready. Itching to draw on connection to build empathy and write something truly special.

The itch might have been the vintage wool, tickling at her wrists. Still, channelling Katharine Hepburn couldn't hurt.

Over the big band now blasting in her ears, she heard a clock tower bell boom nearby. Aware that her attention was skipping like a needle over a broken record, Adelaid hitched her bags higher on her shoulder, gathered every lick of moxie she had at her disposal and strode purposefully through those doors.

Only to rock to a halt the moment she spilled out the other side. For if the exterior of the Big Think Corp was an architectural wonder, the inside was simply dazzling.

From the wall of smoky glass showcasing the view over the Paris end of Collins Street, to the acre of inlaid marble covering the lobby floor, to the sumptuous leather couches and elegant tables and potted white flowers dotting the extravagant three-storey atrium, it had an Art Deco sensibility that she adored. If Big Think Corp headquarters had been designed to inspire shock and awe, it worked.

Adelaid's phone buzzed through her earbuds, jerking her into the present. A quick glance at the screen showed a new message on the Adams family chat.

Jake: Sunday lunch canned. Joey brought gastro home from kinder.

Avatars belonging to all four of her brothers immediately popped up with responses.

Brad: Inconsiderate of him.

Bill: Better you than me.

Sid: Gross.

"Ms Adams?"

Adelaid looked up to find Audrey Hepburn—if Audrey Hepburn was taller, curvier, in her late twenties and had a penchant for tiny wrist tattoos—standing before her.

"Hi! Yes! Adelaid. That's me!" she said, sliding her phone, messages unanswered, and her earbuds into her handbag.

Then she rummaged through her work tote to find the printout of her official invitation. As provided by Big Think's flashy new PR firm, who happened to employ Adelaid's best friend, Georgette, who'd wangled Adelaid the fantasy opportunity, for which she would be forever grateful.

"Don't mind all that," said Audrey II. "No one gets in without us knowing exactly who they are. My name is Hadley. Welcome to Big Think."

Hadley passed Adelaid a lanyard hooked to a

visitor pass sporting a recent photo and her name, spelled correctly, which only elevated Adelaid's impression of the place.

"So, you're interviewing our Ted," said Hadley, beckoning over her shoulder as she sashayed away at a fast clip.

"I am." Curling the lanyard around her neck, Adelaid followed.

"Most journos have their sights set on the other two."

Adelaid had no doubt, for "the other two" were none other than Ronan Gerard—the brains of the operation, of the richer-than-Midas Gerards— and ex-football star and one time Australian of the Year, Sawyer Mahoney—the brawn of the group, though it was, as yet, a little unclear to her what he brought to the endeavour bar a sexy smile and celebrity.

"That's partly why I'm so keen to profile Mr Fincher," said Adelaid.

There wasn't all that much out there about the guy, apart from his incredible success in the field of medical research. Basically, a science nerd with the benefit of more funding at his disposal than the GDP of most small countries, he'd also seemed the least intimidating of the three. Win-win!

"Clever choice," said Hadley. "I wonder what you'll make of his lair."

"Lair?"

Hadley shot Adelaid a smile over her shoulder

as she made a beeline for the opposite corner of the ocean of marble. Which, under foot, did not sound or feel like marble at all.

"The Batcave," said Hadley, waggling her fingers. Then, noticing Adelaid's vintage brogues testing the floor as she walked, said, "Did you know the building is carbon negative? The flooring, for instance, is recycled. Throughout the entire building. Impressive, no?"

"No. I mean, yes. It's…" Adelaid's gaze grazed the vertigo-inducing balconies looking down from the first two floors of office space above. "Fantastical. I feel as if I've stepped thirty years into the future."

That earned Adelaid a Mona Lisa smile.

"Before I send you up," said Hadley, "would you care for a self-guided tour of the building? We provide disposable degradable headphones and an app, as well as an upgrade to your visitor card to allow you access to the relevant areas."

Adelaid's Spidey-senses tingled. A tour would be the physical version of a press release. And pretty much everything she'd read about the company had been cannibalised, repurposed from elegantly curated tales of origin and purpose that could be found on the company website.

She was after something richer. Deeper. Something honest and real.

Connections and empathy. That was her intention.

Someone else could look after carbon.

Fingers stimming over the corner of her visitor pass, Adelaid said, "Another time. I want to be ready for Mr Fincher when he's ready for me."

A quick flick of Hadley's gaze seemed to take in the whole of her, from the fluff of her curly braid to her op shop suit, before she said, "But will he be ready for the likes of you?"

Before Adelaid could make heads or tails of that, they reached the lifts.

Clicking her hand towards Adelaid's visitor pass, Hadley mimed for Adelaid to swipe it over a small square panel in the wall after which the lift doors opened on a quiet swish.

Adelaid stepped inside. "Where to?"

"Your pass has been set to two stops, the Batcave, and the lobby." Then, as the lift doors closed, Hadley added, "Good luck."

The doors closed and the lift was off and away before Adelaid could say thank you.

As the lift hurtled her skyward, she tapped into sensory techniques she'd learned in her teens, to help snag her attention before it strayed too far too fast. She noted a subtle scent of orange blossom, and the whir of electricity through her feet. Found herself wondering what Ted Fincher's quirk might be, maybe a daffy number of lab coats?

Her phone buzzed again, yanking her out of her exercise. She couldn't deal with her brothers right now.

They were not yet privy to the fact she'd quit her job to "follow her dream," and she planned to keep it that way till the profile had found a home. The last thing she needed was their united disappointment, or concerns it was something their mum would have done.

In some deep, unspoiled place inside of her, she hoped they might see the risk as ballsy and brave. Proof that after all her challenges, she'd turned out okay. More than okay. That she was flourishing.

Connections and empathy, she reminded herself as the tone of the lift changed.

Adelaid looked to the display to see which floor she'd reached to find not a number, but the initials *TF*. Suddenly her hopes for a daffy number of lab coats didn't seem likely.

When the doors slid open on a satisfying whoosh, the first thing she noticed was the quiet. No voices, no tapping keyboards, no music, no people bustling by. As someone who needed white noise in order to function, the stillness made her twitch.

The next thing she noticed was the space. For as far as she could tell, Ted Fincher had the entire floor.

Outside the lift doors sat a couple of caramel leather couches, like those downstairs, more plants, a table with notepads and a neat grouping of sharpened pencils and a coat rack. A black freestanding wall had been propped behind them, in the centre a massive framed Carl Sagan quote.

Somewhere, something incredible is waiting to be known.

"Hello?" she called out, her voice barely carrying. Then, "Mr Fincher? Ted?"

No answer.

Curiosity piqued, she poked her head around the wall to find herself in a cross between Leonardo da Vinci's workshop, Dr Strange's mansion and, yep, the Batcave.

The deeper she went, the more dedicated spaces she found. A library with a cosy reading nook. A row of meeting rooms in green glass and blond wood. Arrays of super-tech that would blow her brothers' minds, including VR set-ups with requisite floor space. By the windows at the far end of the floor, three beautiful telescopes of varying sizes stood regally, pointed towards the sky, and in what felt like the centre of the space, a massive bronze globe hung like a chandelier.

The kookiness spoke to her own eclectic sensibilities, but it also had a hermetic, dust-free kind of symmetry. Every notebook lined up with every pencil, every chair was tucked in, as if everything had been placed exactly where the owner wanted it to be. Which was definitely not her.

A sound scraped along the edge of her wildly overstimulated mind, and she flinched.

"Hello?" she called. Then again, after her voice cracked the first time, "Mr Fincher?"

There was a shift of paper, the shuffle of fabric. Then a deep, gravelly voice called out, "Come on through. I'll be with you in a second."

Adelaid hitched the straps of her multiple bags and moved carefully around a maze of cabinets containing awesome collectibles. Geological wonders and old medical equipment and a life-sized replica of Han Solo trapped in carbonite—at least she assumed it was a replica—

"Oh," she gasped when she found herself facing a real live man, sitting at a drafting table.

Maybe it was the simplicity of the man jotting notes using a cheap pencil and dime a dozen notebook, the slightly crooked glasses, the analogue watch sitting low on his wrist.

Maybe it was the way light bounced perfectly off the globe above, creating a cascading golden glow over his outline, making the man appear as if he possessed some magical inner warmth.

Or maybe it was the sheer size of him—huge shoulders, thick neck, legs like tree trunks, scruffy stubble. Like Beauty's Beast might have looked in suit pants and a pale blue button-down.

Add overlong dark auburn hair, aquiline nose, a dark, long-sleeved T-shirt doing its best to contain more muscles than Adelaid knew by name and roping veins jerking in his forearms as he sketched, the man was Marvel-level gorgeous.

Aquiline? some voice queried in the back of her head. She didn't even know what *aquiline* meant, only that it had sprung, unbidden, from some ancient place inside of her that spoke to classic hotness. As if even her ancestors were impressed.

Then he placed the pencil on the table. Neatly. Lining it up with the edge of his notebook. Before his big, squared-off fingers pushed his sleeves higher at his elbows. And he turned to face her, a welcoming smile already in place.

Only when his gaze met hers, he stilled. His muscles jerking, his jaw clenching. His eyes a rich warm molten brown behind the glints of his lenses.

Adelaid's mouth dried up at the sight of him. Completely and utterly. To the point she had to prise her tongue from the roof of her mouth in order to breathe.

Then he blinked, as if coming out of a daydream.

And Adelaid's lungs whimpered in gratitude when she'd remembered to fill them again.

The man pushed his glasses higher on his nose, pressed back his chair and stood, showing off the kind of tall that came with breadth. And heft. And all of it seemed to be in Vitruvian proportion.

"Ted Fincher?" she asked. For she had to be sure before she started wasting so many good words on the man.

He nodded. Then in a voice so deep that she felt it in the backs of her knees, the man said, "Hi."

Adelaid reminded herself that this was a moment that required a surplus of attention rather than her usual deficit. Her only chance to make a good first impression on the man who held all her eggs in his basket. So to speak. She took the final few steps the man's way, smiled and held out a hand—straight arm, strong thrust.

"Mr Fincher," she said. "I'm so happy to meet you."

Katharine Hepburn would have been proud.

One second Ted's heart was doing as it ought: beating a neat fifty-six beats a minute, pushing oxygen-rich blood to his body's tissues, before drawing the oxygen-poor blood back again, ready for nourishment.

The next it forgot its very purpose. Seeming to hover inside his chest cavity, like a lump of wobbly gristle, before finally going back to keeping him alive.

The only possible justification for the aberration was the apparition before him. A wild-haired, pink-cheeked, bright-eyed, fidgety woman, who seemed to crackle with energy even while standing still.

Though, at second glance, she wasn't standing still. She rocked from foot to foot, her hand outstretched, as if waiting…

Waiting for him to shake it.

Ted nudged his glasses higher on his nose, took a step her way and took her by the hand.

He tracked the musculature, the bones, the ridges of knuckle and skin. Everything was where, and as, it should be. And yet…that spark; as if some kind of electrical impulse had leapt from her hand to his, or vice versa. That was new.

He felt the relaxing of her grip, a sign that she was ready to end the holding. Not that they were *holding hands*. A handshake was not at all the same thing. Yet when Ted pulled his hand back into his personal space, he cupped it, the flat tip of his thumb pressing against the sensations playing havoc with his nerves.

"I'm sorry," he said, his voice rough from underuse. How long had it been since he'd spoken aloud to another human being? Hours? Days? "Who did you say you were?"

He was ready this time, when her gaze met his. Braced. Her eyes were wide, lovely and a pale alchemical green. A colour that eyes should not be. Not if someone wanted to be able to look at a person without staring.

"I didn't say, did I?" she said. That *voice*. Breathy and full. Then hand to heart she said, "I'm Adelaid Adams, one 'e,' and I am so excited we get to do this together."

"One 'e'?"

Do what, exactly?

"The 'e' is in the middle," she said, writing her name in the air between them, "not the end." Then, remembering the lanyard around her neck, she took another step closer and lifted it so he could see.

Close enough he noted a mass of tiny curls twisting away from her head, a smattering of freckles on the bridge of her fine nose, the sharp bow of her top lip.

Who was she? He didn't remember her name attached to any of his rigorously guarded slate of projects. Not that he was concerned, as such. She'd never have made it to this floor without getting past Hadley. He was curious. So he let himself off the leash, just a smidge.

And asked, "What exactly are we doing together?"

Her eyes flickered, long tangled lashes sweeping shadows over her cheekbones. "A series of interviews? Me writing a profile on you? You—" She paused to swallow. "You didn't know I was coming."

Ted ran hand up the back of his neck. "Are you sure you weren't after Sawyer? Or Ronan?"

"Nope," she said. "I'd much prefer you."

"If only they were here to hear you say that my year would be made," he said. Only to hear his own words bounce back at him on delay. It sounded like flirting. Was he flirting? It had been a while since he'd partaken in the practice. And never while working.

Working.

He glanced over his shoulder at the desk, at the work he'd been focussed on for the past several hours. Work that had fled from his head the moment he'd seen Adelaid Adams standing before him. He noted the papers he'd mussed up by sitting on them and pulled himself back to standing so that he might tuck them back into a neat pile.

"Hadley," Adelaid said, "gave me this pass. In case you're worried I'm some kind of burglar intent on stealing any of your fancy stuff. Or… mussing up your pencils."

His gaze shot back to hers. Was she flirting now? Or just funny? Her expression seemed… friendly. Curious.

The resultant whoosh had him wondering when he'd last eaten. Or had any water.

He said, "I'm not sure pencil mussing comes under the purview of the burglar."

A glint of mischief lit those mercurial eyes. "And yet, once they get a load of those neat lines and sharp points, the urge might overcome them."

The word *urge* backed up inside his head. Along with *flirt. Staring. Lips. Spark.*

And he wondered, honestly, how long it had been since he'd had an interaction with a human person that did not involve statistics, or study results, or funding.

Long enough he'd let her stand there, carrying what looked to be an inordinate number of heavy bags, for too long.

"Forgive me." Ted looked about, found a stool and carried it to her. Placing it by her. Close enough to catch a waft of berries, of something light and sweet, like icing sugar.

He backed up, giving her space, inviting her to sit. To stay.

Which she did, with a quick smile, wincing as her bags slid from her shoulder and slumped to the floor at her feet. As she pulled her phone free, a flutter of flyaway blond hair wafted over her face before she shot a gust of air from the corner of her mouth to blow it back into place. He was fairly sure she'd had no idea she'd done so.

And when those huge wild green eyes of hers once again found his, heat rushed to his face, while goosebumps rushed down his arms. It was a temperature-controlled space, meaning his re-action had to be due to adrenaline. Fight or flight. Not that he had any intention of doing either.

Attempting to exhibit some measure of self-control, Ted settled back into his own seat, and asked, "What will this involve? If you don't mind me asking."

Snapping the button, rhythmically, on her phone case, she said, "Ask anything you'd like. I don't want this to feel like an interrogation. More like…a conversation."

As she spoke, her right leg started bouncing up and down. Making him wonder if regular movement, for her, was the norm rather than an exception.

"A conversation," he encouraged.

"Exactly! My aim is to give readers a glimpse into other people's lives. To showcase what makes the subject unique but also what makes them the same. So, in your case, I'd love to know more about your work, as well as the man behind the glasses."

Her focus shifted, intensifying, travelling over his face, down his neck, pausing on his chest a moment, before lifting quickly back to his eyes. Her hair fluttering slightly as if she'd sucked in too quick a breath.

"For what purpose?" he asked.

"The profile? The pursuit of connection. And empathy." A shrug. "To get there, as per the rather vociferous contract negotiated with your rabidly intense lawyers, we will catch up several times over the next weeks. There will likely be phone calls, emails, for clarification as we go. And you look dubious."

He felt it. All over. Which was why such appointments usually went Sawyer's way, or Ronan's. He'd much rather do the work than talk about it.

As if she sensed it, she picked at her thumbnail, before seeming to come to a decision. "I'm not here to write an exposé, or delve into anything you decide is too personal. My jam is the weird and the wonderful, their whys and where-fores—as I believe it encourages open minds. Understanding. Acceptance. And I think… I've *seen* how so much of that has been lost of late. Paths of information are narrowing when they ought to be opening up."

A smile, a shrug. Then another long moment in which she simply looked at him, before she shook her head and said, "And I get that people might find your compatriots easier to write about. The magnate and the football star. Please," she scoffed, though there was a glimmer of humour in her eyes. "Do they have multiple PhDs? Are they out there curing diseases? Or making names for themselves regards the Glasgow accords? All that wrapped up in—"

Her words stopped, but her hand kept going—flapping at him, all of him, as if intimating he was as impressive as his résumé.

Then, when she seemed to realise what she had implied, she pulled back her hand, before lifting a bottom cheek and sitting on her fingers.

It was enough to make Ted's head swim. In fact, it *was* swimming. And his belly—it was rumbling. Hollow. How long *had* it been since he'd eaten? Seriously? This light-headedness was not normal.

"Now I've said enough, and this is not meant to be about me, so how about we pick a time for our first proper chat. One day this week?" She turned her phone, finger flicking over the screen to find her calendar, then looked to him in anticipation.

"Thursday," he said, picking a day at random that was long enough away to find out what was actually going on.

"Perfect. First thing?"

He nodded. Knowing he just had to say the word and Ronan would make it go away. For the work came first. Their mission far too important to brook distractions. Though the thought of Adelaid Adams walking out of here and never seeing her again—

"Great!" she said, hopping off the stool and grabbing her gear, then slipping her phone into one of her plethora of bags. When she stood, wisps of hair floated around her like a halo.

Ted pressed finger and thumb into his eye sockets, before running a hand over his chin, feeling the rasp of whiskers against his palm. How long had it been since he'd *shaved*?

Adelaid wavered. "Do you have any questions for me, before I go?"

Are you single?

What's your favourite colour?

How do you take your coffee?

Where do you store all that excess energy and can I have some?

Are you happy?

Would you like to have dinner with me sometime?

Ted shook his head. "Let's save it for Thursday."

Once he'd shaved, and eaten, and guzzled a gallon of water. And seen sunlight. And tidied his desk. And no longer had the scent of her every time he breathed in. Like berries and sugar. Like cake. No, like *muffin*. Heaven help him, Adelaid Adams smelled like a blueberry muffin.

"Okey-doke," she said, then turned to leave. Stopping when she realised she wasn't sure which way she'd come in.

"I'll walk you to the lift."

"Still afraid I might steal something?" She looked back over her shoulder as if checking he was still following. Which he was. Tugged by a thread in his chest yanking him forward.

"Afraid you might get lost. I've been told my plan for the place makes little sense to anyone else."

"I like it," she said. "It's like Disneyland—a new world around every corner." She turned and, walking backwards, held out her phone. "Do you mind if I grab your details? For some reason, your lawyers wouldn't blithely hand over your phone number, home address, mother's maiden name..."

He reached out, his fingers almost brushing hers as he slid the phone from her hand. *Almost.* And still he felt that spark, like an echo of her life force, a tingle in his fingertips as he tapped in his mobile number, his private email and a couple of other ways of getting hold of him. Just in case.

She smiled her thanks when he handed back her phone. After which she tapped in a message, his phone in his back pocket buzzing. "Now you have mine. If you need to get in touch. About anything. Any time."

A flush of pink rose to her cheeks. Blushing being the physiological response to an emotional stimulus.

Their gazes held a mite longer than polite, before she blinked and looked away.

They walked the rest of the way in silence.

At the lift, he leaned past her, waving his card over the sensor pad. Notes of berries making his head spin.

She glanced up. "I'm really looking forward to getting to know you, Ted. You're going to be so glad you did this. Hand to heart, I will not mess it up."

He saw the moment she wished she could take those final words back. A widening of her eyes, a twisting of her full mouth, before she breathed deep and tipped her chin; as if daring him to contradict her.

Which was when all that crackling, compelling nervous energy began to make sense.

Bravado had brought her here. *Gumption*, as Ronan would say. Ronan would like her, Ted thought. Then the thought of Ronan *liking* Adelaid Adams made him feel as if he had heartburn.

As hunger and friction and exhaustion and attraction and the tightening of the rubber band that kept him tied to his desk coalesced into a tight knot inside of his hollowed-out belly, Ted held out a hand. "Till Thursday."

Adelaid hitched her bags before taking his hand in hers. Holding it for a beat. Then a few more.

The lift doors opened and she sprang back, as if caught doing something untoward. But then, before stepping inside the lift, Adelaid reached out, and nudged the notebooks and pencils on the table by the Carl Sagan wall till they sat askew.

"There," she said, grinning, "that's better."

Then she bounded into the lift, and lifted her hand in a wave as the doors closed.

Ted saw his own hand lifted in response in the reflection of the closed doors. He let it drop. While the very room seemed to settle with a sigh now that she was gone.

"What the hell was that?" he said, his voice rough.

Now that he was alone, now that he could think, all evidence pointed to mitigating circumstances. A man of his size had specific fuel requirements. He'd been known to hallucinate entire conversations when he lost track of time, when the work was going well.

Once he'd called Sawyer to ask his advice on where they might set up a lab in Sydney, only to find it was three in the morning, and Sawyer was in Bolivia. And then there was the time he was sure he'd seen Ronan and Hadley making out in a broom closet at a party in their pre–Big

Think days, which they'd assured him, vociferously, he had not.

Turning, Ted lumbered back to his desk—but not before quickly tidying the notebooks and pencils—and finished off the notes he'd been making before he'd been interrupted.

He took out his phone to put in a call to their executive chef—one of the better additions Ronan had insisted upon when they'd built the place— he found a new message. From a new number.

Ted, this is Adelaid. One "e", see! Looking forward to Thursday. And don't worry, if anyone can ferret out the weird and the wonderful, it's me. All you have to do is show up.

He slid the message away, put in an order for a lot of steamed chicken and vegetables, then dropped to the floor and did as many push-ups as his body would allow, in the hopes of returning to some level of normal.

CHAPTER TWO

"ARE WE READY?" asked Ronan as he strode into the Big Think founders' private meeting room—less fancy boardroom, more like the university lounge in which Ted, Ronan and Sawyer had first met.

Ronan headed straight to his corner of the room, the chair he'd brought in rather reminiscent of a throne.

"Ready," Ted concurred, grabbing sushi bites from the tray Hadley had asked the chef to whip up, and dropping into his battered blue lounger in the corner.

The chair had been his dad's. After his dad's sudden passing, he'd dragged the thing back to uni, and it had come with him ever since. A touchstone. A reminder as to what he was doing with his life and why.

"Ready," Hadley agreed, leaning in the doorway like some kind of upmarket bouncer, an edge to her voice, as if having to sound off to Ronan was beneath her.

If Sawyer was in town, he'd be pulling up a random chair, turning it backwards, straddling the thing and tossing something from hand to hand.

"Talk," said Ronan, waving a hand like a Jedi.

"Ted had a girl in his lair." That was Hadley.

Ted flinched so hard he pulled a muscle in his neck.

"What girl?" Ronan barked.

"Not a girl," said Ted. "A woman."

A lanky blonde with pink cheeks and a habit of nibbling her bottom lip. He'd thought about that bottom lip, the way she'd messed up his pencils, her sweet scent, far too often in the days since. It had been distracting. Enough he planned to fix it, in this meeting. One hundred percent.

"Her name was Adelaid Adams," Ted added when the others continued staring at him. "One 'e.' She's a journalist." Then, seeing where he'd actually gone wrong, added, "If that was to whom you were referring."

"You let a journalist get to Ted?" That, from Ronan.

Hadley bristled in Ronan's direction. "You're the one who insisted upon some outside PR after lamenting that our press was beginning to stagnate. 'We need to be humanised,' you said, right here in this room. 'Given the warm and fuzzy treatment.'"

"That last part does not sound at all like me."

A shrug. "Either way, the PR mob have been proficient, if overzealous. I sifted through the hundreds of requests to interview *you* and winnowed them down to a couple of dozen."

A slight bow of thanks.

"Nearly as many are ready for Sawyer, when he's able. But Ms Adams requested Ted. So, I looked into her. Melbourne uni. Earned her master's part-time while also working for a light online ezine with big numbers. But it's her side hustle I like—writing longer form features for community papers. Open-minded, insightful, clever with a lovely edge of dry humour. Nice fit for our Ted."

Hadley shot Ted a smile, reminding him of a Venus flytrap.

If was enough to have Ted shifting in his seat. He wondered if Adelaid's fidgets were due to sugar levels, or sudden strange feelings and needing somewhere to put them.

Not that he'd get the chance to find out, for there was an eighty-five percent chance he was putting a stop to the whole thing. If Ronan didn't put a stop to it first.

Then Ronan said, "Things are chilly out there. Purses are tight. A new angle might help. Ted?"

Leaving Ted seventy-three percent sure they'd not blink if he asked not to do the interview.

But Ronan was right. For all that their start-up capital had been immense, their turnover eye-watering, the kinds of projects Ted was determined to see through—curing every damn kind of cancer on the planet, and that was just the start—needed more. And more. And more.

"Whatever you need," he found himself saying. "I'll make sure it doesn't interfere with the work."

Hadley reached over and patted his knee. "Let her interfere, Ted. Might do you some good."

Ronan coughed out a laugh, then covered it with a stately clearing of the throat. "Hard to imagine, but our Ted had game, once upon a time. Girls on campus would flock towards him, in droves, cartoon love hearts beating out of their eyes."

Hadley looked to Ted, a newfound glint in her eye. "Ted was a playa?"

Ted shrugged it off. Not a player—tall, clean-cut and a good listener adept at balancing work, study, family, girls. Till he'd taken a gap year, mid-degree, and his whole world had flipped on its head. His priorities shifting so drastically "game" had been the last thing on his mind.

"Come to think of it," said Hadley, "I am often hit up by women making wildly inappropriate offers in order to be seated at Ted's table at Big Think fundraisers. If I knew you were up for it, Ted, I could be filthy rich by now."

Ted held up a hand. "Thanks all the same."

Hands raised in submission, Hadley glanced at Ronan, smirking when Ronan's eye twitched with the effort not to ask how many women had asked the same about him.

Then Ronan waved a hand, done with the conversation. And he moved onto the minutiae of running their company.

Leaving Ted to figure out how to manage the Adelaid situation, now that it wasn't going away.

Chemistry could explain the flush of hormones that led to an unnatural feeling of euphoria, biology the inclination to ensure the propagation of the species, and physics the attraction of materials, specifically unpaired electrons spinning in the same direction.

He was currently unpaired. Had been for some time. His relationships fizzling out rather quickly due to a lack of time. One ex claiming she'd have had better luck if he'd found her at the bottom of a Petrie dish.

Adelaid's "pairing" status was unknown. Perhaps *trusting* that she was paired would negate the physics. Tipping a portion of control back in his favour. Though, like his initial conclusions, it was untested or peer reviewed.

"That it, then?" Hadley asked.

"Somewhere better to be?" Ronan asked.

"Always," she said, shooting him a saccharine smile before shooting out the door.

Ted hauled himself from his dad's lounger, gave the arm a quick pat, saluted Ronan and left.

On his way to their private lift, Ted pulled out

his phone, and opened a secure, well-sourced search engine the three of them had invested in during their university days, the huge success helping them make their first million as a team.

He typed *The science of attraction.*

Before meeting Adelaid again, Ted intended to arm himself. It was time to hit the books.

Adelaid strode up Collins Street, drinking in the gothic architecture glistening with the wash of recent rain, Gene Kelly skiting about his excellent rhythm via her earbuds.

She adored this part of Melbourne. *Grace* Kelly would have fit right in, swanning past the glamorous designer shops. In fact, she'd had Grace in mind when pinning a black velvet flower to her French twist and donning a collarless shirt with capped sleeves and ruching across the torso, tucked into a black crepe poodle skirt that swished as she walked.

She'd sent her revised pitch—complete with Ted's shiny new release form—to her top editors, publications and websites. Now all she had to do was wait for the bidding war to ensue, and the whole thing to go down in folklore. Oh, and interview Ted Fincher several times and write the thing, and keep hustling for extra work on the side so she could pay her rent.

At the very least she could be grateful not to be sitting at her old hot desk, mainlining dodgy drip coffee and trying to find a new angle from which to talk about period cups and K-pop.

Her phone buzzed in her ears. She checked in case it was Ted; alas it was the Adams family group chat.

Jake: Sunday lunch back on. False alarm.

Sid: Can't, working, booked in a big new job.

Brad: Go get 'em.

Jake: Great work, mate. Addy, bring chicken wings.

Nose scrunched at her phone, Adelaid considered copying and pasting Sid's message.

Can't, working, booked in a big new job.

It would be the truth, after all. But whereas for Sid it was all pats on the back, for her it would only bring down an avalanche of questions. A broken record of big brotherly worry.

She would wait till she had real news. Irrefutably fabulous news. Till then it was full steam ahead, following her dreams!

When Adelaid reached the café, she quickly checked to see if Ted had beaten her there. While she'd learned to manage most other symptoms of her condition relatively well, her relationship with time remained tense. When there was no sign of him, she tipped her earbuds from her ears and slipped them into their case, the white noise of the café lifting around her.

Only to leap from her shoes when she heard a familiar deep voice right behind her say: "Adelaid Adams."

She spun, the soul of her ballet flat catching on a tile, knocking her off balance. She grabbed for the only thing within reach to stop herself from falling on her backside. She grabbed Ted.

Ted's shirt to be exact, her fingers gripping, slipping and ripping, an opalescent button flying past her nose.

The world took a moment to stop spinning. A moment in which Adelaid realised Ted had caught her, his big strong arms holding her in something akin to a Hollywood dip. While her fingers gripped his torn shirt and his meaty shoulder respectively with all she had.

He'd shaved, she noticed, now she was up close and personal. Gone was the scruff from the day they'd met, and in its place, granite jaw, and cheekbones, and wide kissable lips.

Kissable? They were just lips. There, ready to do whatever other things lips did.

Moving away from his lips, she noticed his glasses were different from last time too, though still slightly crooked. No, not his glasses, his nose. There was a bend, as if it had been broken at some point. Though, instead of marring what was an otherwise impossibly beautiful collection of features, right up there with the likes of Paul Newman, and Montgomery Clift, that nose gave him an edge. Grit. The kind that planted a seed in a woman's belly, and before she knew it there were vines twirling about her inside, every which way.

Ted's hand at her waist gripped a smidge tighter, his fingers digging into her side in a way that made all kinds of warm sparkly feelings tumble through her.

She realised, belatedly, he was only readying to pull her upright. Her body lifted to land flush against his. Putting her eyes level with the second buttonhole which was now devoid of a button, the shirt pulling open a smidge so that she was looking at a patch of warm male skin.

"Oops," she managed, her fingers sliding to the offending spot and attempting to tug the fabric together.

"It's fine," he rumbled in a cavernous voice that vibrated through her. "Are you okay?"

She looked up, and up, and up. "I'm fine. Mortified, but fine. You?"

He lifted a hand to cover hers, which was when she realised she hadn't stopped playing with the gap in his shirt. Fiddling was par for the course

for her, fiddling with other people something to
be avoided, at least without prior permission.

Mortification deepening, she stepped back,
arching away from his embrace, and he let her go.

The moment might have been salvageable, if
not for the flower in her hair choosing that moment to pop free till it dangled over her ear. She
quickly plucked the thing off and shoved it into
a bag.

Ted hadn't missed a moment of her circus act.
And yet, there was no judgement in his gaze.
None of her brother Sid's eye rolls. Or Brad's sigh
of disappointment at seeing her make a klutz of
herself. No flicker of wariness that came over
most new people of her acquaintance during such
moments. Just warm, polite interest. In fact, he
looked so clean cut, so neat and tidy, so big and
unimpeachable, butter wouldn't melt. And yet instinct had her feeling something warm and new
and dangerous arcing between them.

"Shall we sit?" she asked, her voice a little
reedy.

He nodded and held out a hand so that she
might lead him inside.

His gaze burning a hole into her back, she led
him to a semi-private booth that—along with the
cookie dough and fresh coffee scent—would help
them both relax.

Adelaid slid into a seat. Only to find Ted staring at the tight space, as if trying to work out,

mathematically, how he could curl his gargantuan body into the right pretzel shape so that he might fit.

"Oh," she said, holding out a hand. "Hang on, we can move!"

He shook his head, and somehow managed to curl himself between the table and bench. Till he tried to find space for his long legs, only for his ankles to slide along hers.

Adelaid covered it with a quick, apologetic smile, and tucked her feet as far beneath her as they would go, and hoped her pulse would calm the heck down. Not easy when the feel of Ted's arms, and chest, and now leg, had left lasting imprints on her skin.

"What can I get you?"

Adelaid could have kissed the friendly face of the waitress who had popped up beside them. She ordered strong coffee and a piece of the apple rhubarb pie; Ted ordered a fresh squeezed juice and an egg white omelette.

"You sure?" Adelaid asked. "The cakes here are amazing."

"I'd last five minutes before needing to eat again," he said. "The bane of being this big."

The waitress sighed and left. Then it was just the two of them. Sitting across the table from one another, the scent of sugar on the air.

"Let's get this show on the road!"

Adelaid found her phone deep inside the wrong

bag, made sure Ted agreed before turning on the recorder app. Then she reached into her work tote, grabbed a couple of pencils, chose the one that didn't need sharpening and the notebook in which she'd been jotting research and question ideas. A few random sticky notes fluttered to the table, and she shoved them in the back of the notebook.

Once she had everything within reach, she looked up to find Ted leaning his chin on his upturned palm as he took in her mobile office.

He picked up a pencil shaving that must have been stuck to...something, and his eyes met hers. Warm behind his dark-rimmed glasses. She may have swayed a little from the impact.

Adelaid shrugged. "It's...organised chaos."

"It's *pure* chaos."

He laughed as he said it, as if there was wonder behind his comment, not sanction, yet something ugly shifted in Adelaid's chest. Echoes of the multiple times she'd had similar words tossed her way.

"You're late, again."

"Can't you just sit still?"

"Anyone ever told you how tactless you can be? It's frustrating as hell."

But his gaze was curious, kind. Reminding her there was no way he could know he'd poked at a sore spot. And the fact she'd borne witness to the anal—in her opinion—neatness of his workspace, to her mind indicative of its own kind of pathology, helped her settle.

And say, "Yet, for me, it works. Which is what matters, correct?"

A little thinking time, then a nod. "Correct."

"Great. First question. Any subject you'd prefer *not* to touch on?"

"No."

Though a muscle in his jaw ticked, and Adelaid made a mental note to tread carefully till she found *his* sore spot. "What if I'm…an industrial spy? Like Ingrid Bergman in *Notorious*."

"She was a political spy, if I'm not mistaken."

Adelaid blinked. "I can't believe you just corrected me on an old-timey movie. That would be like me correcting you on the chemical formula for…butane."

"C_4H_{10}," he said with a smile in his eyes.

Pencil waggling at the ends of her fingers she said, "How about you tell me your safe word, just in case."

"My *safe word*?" he repeated, gaze glinting, voice dropping.

"*A* safe word," she adjusted, her cheeks warming. "A word you can use that tells me I've pushed too far. We can come up with a new one, you know, in case you have one you use in…other parts of your life."

If only he'd look away, then she might stop babbling. But those eyes of his—all that deep,

soft, warm, inviting, molten, chocolatey brown—
made her ears ring and her pulse throb. Made it
hard to concentrate. And when that was already
an issue for her, she had to work extra hard to
stay on task.

"Adelaid?"

"Mmm?" She came to, to find that she was now
leaning forward too, her pencil tapping madly on
the table. "Look, I'm nice but I'm pushy. Chances
are I will, at some point, wander into a paddock
you think is clearly out of bounds, but unless
there's a great big 'keep off the grass' sign, I'll
stomp all over the place."

He breathed in, slow and deep, the light now
reflecting off his glasses so she could no longer
quite see his eyes. Then he said, "Muffin."

"You'd like a muffin?"

He shook his head, and blinked a couple of
times, as if coming out of a daze.

"Our *safe word* is 'muffin'?" Adelaid's mouth
quirked as she wrote the word on her notebook.
Drawing a cloud around the edges, with little rays
of sunshine bursting out in all directions. "Any
particular kind of muffin?"

She looked up in time to see a muscle ticking
at the edge of his jaw. Then his gaze dropped to
her mouth as he rumbled, "Blueberry."

Oh, my. "Blueberry muffin, it is. Now, let's
start with an easy one. How did you, Sawyer and
Ronan meet?"

Ted finally leaned back, arms moving to cross over his impressive chest. Meaning his legs stretched out further under the table too; a shift of air told her how close his foot was to hers. Unfortunately, she couldn't tuck her legs any deeper under her seat or she'd end up under there herself.

"University."

Adelaid nodded, encouraging him to go on. But he was done. Flicking to a fresh page in her notebook, she wrote down, slowly, in big bold letters, *MET AT UNIVERSITY*, and doodled as she asked, "Were you in the same class?"

"No."

"Same…dorm?"

"No."

She stopped doodling. "Ted. Your origin story is no secret. In fact, it gets an airing in pretty much every Big Think story out there. Sawyer Mahoney, Ronan Gerard and Ted Fincher were best friends at uni. Young Ted—that would be you—"

Ted's eyebrows rose a smidge.

"Became friends with Ronan—a risk taker with an eye for talent. Sawyer one day wandered into a meeting they were having when he thought he smelled cookies. How am I doing?"

"Close." He ran a hand over his chin, and she could all but hear the rasp of fresh stubble against his strong hand. As if the clean-cut look took work. As if the bit of rough she'd seen the other day lived just beneath the surface. "Except the food."

"What was it, then? If you say *blueberry muffin* I might cry."

"Well, we wouldn't want that, now, would we? Not on day one."

She barked out an unexpected laugh. Once again, that unexpected flash of grit getting under her skin. Twirling her pencil, she tried a new angle.

"What did you study at uni?"

"Everything."

Putting aside the buzz of concern that Ted Fincher might actually turn out to be a dud interview, Adelaid reminded herself that *she* was the experienced one in this situation. That it was on her to take control.

"Ted. It might sound contrary, but this will all be over faster if you avoid one-word answers."

He breathed in, his chest rising and falling. And his foot rubbed against hers. The slide of it making her breath hitch. Which he did not miss, as his gaze was locked onto hers.

"Here we go!" said the waitress, leaning between them as she passed out their food. As she turned to leave, she shot Adelaid a look that said, *You go, girl*.

Ted missed it all, as he was already ploughing through his huge omelette. "How about you?" he asked, taking a breath between bites.

"Me?"

"Where did you go to uni?"

"This isn't about me," said Adelaid. First rule of journalism—don't put yourself into the story. "How about insight into some projects you're overseeing?"

"Which?"

She tilted her head. Gave him a look.

He grinned. A flash of big white teeth. And eye crinkles. And mouth brackets. And so many lovely, charming things she found herself a little starstruck.

"Pick one," she said. "I beg you."

This time he laughed, a rich chuckle that rocketed down her spine.

He rearranged his large body again. "I'm not in the habit of talking about myself, Adelaid. Theory, progress, budgets, logistics, with those who are working alongside me, yes. Sawyer is the salesman. Ronan the negotiator. I just—"

"You just...?"

"Do the work."

"So, tell me about that. The work. Tell me something you'd like the world to know about what it is that you do. Help me help you."

He stared at the table for a bit. Then, with a nod, he said, "Okay. When you found me the other day, I was working on something we've dubbed the Noah Project."

Even while her fingers itched to get around a pencil—to scratch out arrows, bubbles, squiggles all over the page, for doodling helped her remake connections when she looked back at her notes, Adelaid didn't move lest she spook him. For once he got started talking about the clean water project they had been working on for the better part of a decade, he was wonderful. Not a dud, not even a tiny little bit.

"I choose projects," Ted said, winding down, "which have meaning to me. It may sound selfish, and it is, to a point, but there also has to be some structure, some finite parameters, or we would be stretched too thin. Success is imperative. Not merely progress but results. I leave the red tape to others to sort out, because the work—whether it be vaccines, or clean water, or disease eradication—is what matters. It's all that matters. And your eyes are glazing over."

Adelaid blinked, realising she'd cradled her coffee at her chest the entire time she'd listened to that rough rumbling voice. Watched his big, elegant hands swish through the air as he became increasingly animated the more he talked about his work. And gazed into those lovely, warm, crinkling, chocolatey eyes.

"No! That was great. Honestly."

Ted's hand moved to the back of his neck. "It was esoteric."

"It was impassioned." Adelaid sat forward, knocking a pencil with her elbow, the thing rolling to the floor. "What's your mission statement?"

His eyebrow kicked north.

"Come on, I know you have one. Written on a napkin or printed on a T-shirt."

His gaze caught on hers, his expression serious as he said, simply, "To save the world."

And there was not a drop of irony attached.

"See," she said, still trying to shake off the dreamy feeling that had come over her. "You're a natural at this. You just needed a little nudge."

He looked at her then, as if trying to figure out if she was making fun.

"Do you know what my favourite part of my job is?" Adelaid asked.

"Stationery," he said, eyes roving over the spread now covering half the table. Eyes still gentle and kind.

"A teeny tiny smidge above stationery," she said, picking up a pencil and writing words and underlining them on the page. "It's the people. People with tall tales, and big dreams, and unique stories. People who surprise me. Who will surprise readers into realising that every single person on the planet has something to offer. A story to tell. A lesson to teach. And enough in common with everyone else that they are worth caring about. Even if that person seems so very different from them. Especially if they seem…"

How to put this?

"More weird than wonderful," said Ted.

Adelaid looked up from her frantic underlining, surprised he'd remembered her exact words.

What was not a surprise was the buzz that came with landing on something real—interview one, day one. The logistics, science, tech and political manoeuvring—all that would elevate the piece. Create hooks on which to sell it.

Ted Fincher wasn't some run of the mill, big, handsome cinnamon roll, genius billionaire. He had edges, reasons, passion. He was the real deal.

"Okay," she said, snapping her notebook closed.

"We're done?"

"For today. Don't want to wear you out."

"Do I look worn out?" His arms once again folded across his insanely broad chest, long blunt fingers curling around meaty forearms. Only this time it wasn't in self-protection.

For the man was smiling, his gaze lit with interest. Curiosity. As if, now that he was fed, he was…switched on.

"I'd booked you in for an hour. It's been closer to two."

Ted jerked, then checked his watch—which meant twisting his arm, the face of the chunky analogue piece having settled over his inner wrist.

"Shall we go?"

He nodded, tidying up his side of the table, which meant lining up knife and fork in perfect parallel.

The waitress was back, flirting with Ted, giving Adelaid time to gather up her accoutrements only to remember the dropped pencil.

She reached out with her shoe. Finding no luck, she shuffled her backside as low as it would go beneath the table, sweeping her foot over the floor, only to feel her skirt bunch in a loud crinkling mass all the way to her hip when her inner thigh brushed right along Ted's.

She froze, balanced precariously on the edge of the seat, her arms straining to hold her in that strange off-kilter position, eyes so wide they began to burn for lack of blinking.

Ted looked cool as a cucumber. As if he sat entangled in women's legs, a knee positioned danger-close, day in day out. He didn't even break eye contact with the waitress, who was now leaning her backside against their table as she told a story about her adorable new niece.

Then he had to go and breathe.

His chest rising, filling deeply, his leg shifted, infinitesimally, towards her. His knee now millimetres from where a man's knee ought not to be. Not till the second date, at least.

Not that this was a date. It was an *interview*, a chance to get to know the man beneath the suit. Not that she was thinking about him that way. *Suit-less*.

Before this went downhill completely, she held her breath, quickly spread her legs wide enough to disengage and then dragged herself back to sitting. Then, feeling itchy, and pink, and hot, and breathless, she made a big to-do of gathering her things.

Enough that the waitress leapt up from the table.

Giving Ted leave to finally look Adelaid's way. His eyes were dark, the edge of his mouth hooked into a smile. "You all right over there?"

"I was trying to find the pencil I dropped earlier. Not…" *Feel you up with my thigh.*

Ted carefully eased himself out from behind the table, bent and came up with her pencil. "Yours?"

"Yep! Thanks." She snagged it from his hand, hooked her bag straps over her shoulder, ran a quick had over her messy hair and slid out of the booth.

"Have a good day now," the waitress sing-songed, and Adelaid jumped, having forgotten she was still there.

Nerves snappy, Adelaid kept up her pace as she led Ted through the café. He reached past her to hold open the door, standing back to wave her through.

Out front, beneath the awning, the day having warmed, the earlier rain giving the air weight, Adelaid clasped her bags against her front. Like a shield.

"You that way?" He glanced down Collins in

the direction of her pointing thumb, away from Big Think. "I'll walk you to your car—"

"No car. I don't drive. Tram. Then train. And I've kept you from saving the world long enough."

A muscle flickered under Ted's eye, too quick for her to guess why. But he nodded.

"I'll message you so that we can set a date for our next chat. Okay?" She was already backing down the street.

He nodded again. All talked out apparently, his one-word answers now down to no-word answers.

"Fair warning," she called, lifting a hand to her mouth, for some reason loath to turn and leave him behind. "I'll not be quite so easy on you next time."

Ted lifted a hand, holding it over his heart, as if shot, then lifted the hand in a wave, that big hand of his half blocking out the sun.

And there he stayed, beneath the twee red gingham awning. She'd have bet quite a bit that if she glanced over her shoulder he'd still be there.

It took every ounce of willpower she had not to look back to check.

"Dammit," he growled, still in the shade of the café awning for a few long moments after Adelaid walked away, even when the sun shining through the squares above began to play hazard with his eyeballs.

The excessive amount of time he'd given over

to learning about the science of attraction prior to today's interview had clearly not helped when it came to navigating it in the field.

Take *muffin*. He'd actually said the word out loud. The scent of it, of her, when he'd held her in his arms in that wildly unexpected moment in the doorway of the café. Berries. And sugar. It made his head go foggy. *She* made his head go foggy.

When his head could not *be* foggy. Ever.

His constancy, his focus, his unimpeachable dedication to the cause, were his greatest assets. It gave him an edge over every other clever scientist out there trying to scrounge for the same fundraising, the same lab time, the same journal space.

He wanted it more.

He lifted his hand to his late father's watch, tugged it till it sat flat against his wrist, reminding himself why that was.

He knew he wasn't the only person out there trying to cure cancer. Or autoimmune diseases. Or Alzheimer's. Or give marginalised communities access to better healthcare. But if he didn't use the assets at his disposal, to his utmost ability, and someone he knew fell ill, and he couldn't help them, then that was on him.

For the rest of his life.

And still he watched Adelaid: the heel-toe walk, the brave set of her shoulders and wild flutter of her hair. The constant adjusting of the strange assortment of bags she seemed to insist on taking with her wherever she went. Finding her endlessly fascinating.

"Enough," he said, then turned to leave right as Adelaid glanced back.

Finding him there, watching her still, she stumbled. Instinct had him reaching for her, though she was a good fifty metres away. He turned it into a wave.

Adelaid shot him a jaunty salute, which brought a smile to his face. And he could only be thankful it wasn't happening anywhere near Sawyer, or Ronan, or gods forbid Hadley, or he'd never hear the end of it.

With that he spun on his heel and headed up the hill, filling his lungs with the scent of wet roads and diesel. Anything but sugar and berries, which, it turned out, were his own particular brand of kryptonite.

Understanding the science hadn't worked. So, what next?

Compartmentalisation. He was *good* at compartmentalising. It was how he was able to juggle as many disparate projects as he did.

Where to put Adelaid?

They weren't colleagues, though they were connected through his work.

They weren't friends, though they were engaging in social interactions, with the main goal to get to know one another. At least hers was to get to know him. While his, apparently, was to gaze at her in wonder while keeping track of her stray stationery.

He could, of course, forget about trying to put her anywhere, grow a backbone and keep these messy damn feelings in check.

Maybe he should just pull the pin. If he needed to get out of a contract, Ronan would make it happen. Ronan would lock down the entire building if that's what Ted needed in order to do the work.

Save the World. Their lofty mission statement promised on a three-way handshake when Ronan, Sawyer and Ted were barely into adulthood, now written out in life-sized letters on the floor of the foyer, for those who worked in their building to see every time they came down in the glass-walled lift.

But he couldn't do it. Couldn't do it to Adelaid. This interview was clearly important to her. Cutting her off would hurt her. And, it turned out, hurting her was simply not an option.

Compartmentalisation, it was.

Decision made, he waited for a break in the traffic and jogged across the road towards the gleaming tower his work had built.

CHAPTER THREE

ADELAID WAS LATE.

Ted rubbed his eyes behind his glasses so that he didn't have to watch the emails leaping into his inbox like lemmings following one another over a cliff.

Somehow, in the past five minutes—minutes during which he ought to have been meeting with Adelaid—a small fire had broken out in the Nice lab, which would now be closed till insurance signed off on repairs, and there had been a staff walkout in the Phoenix lab due to a love triangle between the project manager, a lab assistant and a delivery driver.

It was rare for Ted to wish he'd spent his early years concentrating on cloning, or time travel, so that he could be in all places at all times, but sometimes it felt as if no one else took the work seriously.

Took *his time* seriously.

Fixing his glasses back into his nose, Ted twisted his father's watch, giving the face a quick swipe with the flat of his thumb, before checking the time again.

When another email popped up with the subject heading Black lace panties found in office desk drawer. He forwarded it to Hadley to sort out, knowing she'd relish it.

She responded in seconds.

Brilliant. And she's here. Sending her up now.

Ted pushed his chair back so fast it tipped onto two legs before settling back to earth with a bump. It was time. Time to switch from work Ted to interview Ted.

Compartmentalisation time.

Leaving the email lemmings behind, he jogged to the lift, swiped his ID card and pressed the button for the fifth floor.

As part of the compartmentalisation tactic, he'd suggested Big Think as the location for their next interview. Then called on Hadley to source a spare room in the building. Something large and utilitarian. Blank walls. A large table so there was no chance of accidental footsies. A water cooler, a coffee machine and snacks—he wasn't a barbarian—and excellent ventilation so the space didn't instantly fill with the scent of berries and sugar.

Once in the lift he rolled his neck, stretched out his shoulders, bounced up and down so as to increase the oxygen flow to his brain. Like a prize-fighter going into battle. Only the battle here was with himself.

When the lift door opened, he even had the words *You're late* on the tip of his tongue, but they dried up the moment he saw her, waiting for him in the hall.

Today's getup consisted of woollen pants that swept the floor and sat high on her waist and a sleeveless frilly shirt that showed off lean muscled arms, probably from constantly carrying so many bags, her dark blond waves twirled into some fancy knot at her neck.

"Hi," he said, a smile tugging at his mouth before he even felt it coming.

She spun to face him. And if he pretended not to notice that she too was a little breathless, her cheeks a smidge pink, her green eyes sparking the moment she saw him, then it was all in the name of the cause.

"You look—" Ted stopped himself, realising it would not help to tell her he thought her spectacular.

"Frazzled?" Adelaid ran a hand over her hair, which instantly sprang back into soft fluttery waves. "Sorry I'm late. I was called in last minute to watch my twin nephews for my sister-in-law Betty, so she could go to a doctor's appointment. I adore them, but…wow. You have any?"

"Doctor's appointments?"

She grinned and he felt it like a flaming arrow to the chest.

"Nephews."

He shook his head, marvelling at her energy. She was bottled lightning.

"I have a dozen. Nieces and nephews. Needless to say, I am quite the in-demand babysitter."

"I was going to say you look ready and raring."

"I am that too," she said with another blinding smile. Then looked up and down the empty hall. "Are we in the right place?"

Ted ushered her down the hall, sensor lights brightening their way. "This is, currently, unused space. We designed the building with a view to the future. To expansion. To giving back. We have several floors dedicated to free space for use by innovative young entrepreneurs, so that they might spend all their time, energy, money on the work."

"Look at you go, selling the place."

Ted shot her a look. "This looks like the spot," he said when they reached an open door. Inside he found coffee, snacks, water, as requested. Along with his favourite notebooks and pencils, lined up in neat rows.

Adelaid noticed, and gave him a sly smile, before heading in and choosing a chair.

Ted chose another at minimum safe distance, took out his phone, put it on silent, facedown.

Adelaid, on the other hand, emptied her tote

bag, spread out her things, made piles of seemingly random scraps of paper, and coloured things, and joining bits. To him it looked like everything had been tossed about willy-nilly. Yet Adelaid sighed in satisfaction. The sound curling about his insides like smoke.

Then her gaze found his. "I know it looks a mess," she said, "as if there is no rhyme or reason, but it's—"

"Colour-coded, right?"

A blink, then, "Right."

"Ronan works the same way. Sawyer bought him a set of pastel highlighters for his last birthday. He acted as if he could not think of anything more ridiculous, but those things get a lot of use."

Adelaid grinned. Frowned. Then grinned again. Her energy fluctuating with such rapidity, such animation, Ted felt as if he had a sudden case of vertigo.

Then she breathed out hard and said, "Let's go. Are you a Theodore?"

Ted said, "Blueberry muffin."

Adelaid burst into laughter. A bark, husky and dry. Then she leaned forward, her hand reaching towards him. "Hang on, are you serious? That's the hill you choose to die on?"

He shook his head. "I am a Theodore. Full name Theodore Grosvenor Fincher. All family names."

"I'd hope so," she shot back, grinning now as

she wrote his name in big bold strokes in the middle of a half-used page, drawing a big starburst around the lot. Adding shading. And little fireworks.

"Can I call you Teddy?" she asked, pencil tapping against her bottom lip.

"Not if you expect me to answer." When he found himself staring at her mouth, Ted shot from the chair and moved to the coffee station. Maybe the compartments ought to have been physical. The both of them seated easier either side of a wall.

He lifted a coffee cup in question. She answered with a nod.

"How about you?" he asked. "You ever get Addy?"

"Often," she said, pencil now rolling between her lips. "I have had *many* nicknames in my lifetime. Four older brothers made sure of that."

"I'm sorry, did you say four?"

"Yup. So whatever you might come up with, it's been done."

"You tell me yours and I'll tell you mine."

Her eyes narrowed as she considered. Then, curiosity getting the better of her, she said, "Shortcake. Blondie. Devil Incarnate. I was pretty wild as a kid. Knock-Knock, as in Who's There? Complete with tap on the forehead. You?"

"Chrysler," he said, "as in the building. I was six feet tall by the time I was twelve. Six-four by the time I was fourteen, which led to Optimus, as in Prime. When the glasses came on board, Kent."

"As in… Clark?"

"That's the one."

Her gaze roved over him then, unimpeded. As if deciding whether or not it fit. When her teeth tugged on her bottom lip and she let go a soft sigh he figured her a Superman fan.

Then she frowned, and grabbed her pencil, and began drawing random squiggles on her notebook. "Mine were *all* obnoxious, while yours were positive assertions as to your—"

"My…?"

She waved a hand at him, up and down, as if it was obvious.

A voice in the back of his head told him to press, but he had asked Hadley to put them in this dull white room for a reason.

He finished making their coffees, passed hers to her, then sat back down.

"So," she said, her gaze now serious. "I'm thinking we go warm and fuzzy today. Save deep and meaningful for when we know one another better."

Ted winced. "What's behind door number three?"

"You'll do fine. Imagine, if you will, the kinds of stories they always put at the end of the news."

"Such as?"

"Ah, ever rescued a dog lost at sea?"

"Not that I recall."

"Pity. How about a little old lady from a house fire? No? A cat up a tree?"

"Don't be fooled by the glasses, I'm usually locked up in the lair rather than out in the world, ears cocked for cries of distress."

"Mmm. I don't know about that. If half of what I've read about you is true the glasses are no disguise at all." She shuffled on her chair and a hank of hair that had fallen from the twist fell over one shoulder, giving off serious Lana Turner vibes. "Ted, your work is nothing short of heroic. It's my job to balance that out with a little everyday down-to-earth stuff. Or readers might swoon themselves into a stupor."

"Swoon. Into a stupor."

She waved a hand at him, once again as if that was simply obvious. If he wasn't careful, she was going to give him a complex.

"Help me out here!" she begged. "Something funny from the lab? Have you accidentally torn a hole in the space-time continuum? Or genetically crossed a chicken and a goat?"

He lifted a hand. "Now we are treading close to proprietary information."

She laughed again. The sound husky, and raw. Scraping against his insides like fingernails down his chest. Like her fingernails, when she'd played with the hole in his shirt. The hole *she'd* torn.

"Chick-goats hidden in some secret lab?" she asked.

Jaw tight, Ted shook his head. "No goat-kens, either."

"Disappointing," she said. "So, no rescues. No lab accidents. How about—? No." She stopped, her voice catching on a husky note. Her gaze darkening. Her fingers running up and down her pencil. Before she blinked madly and looked to her notebook where she was suddenly taken with doodling little waves.

"How about?" he encouraged, even while he heard the sirens warming up inside his head.

She took a breath and looked up. Looked him dead in the eye. "I was going to ask, for the warm and fuzzy angle, if you were, perhaps, seeing anyone."

Her eyes were overbright as they held his. As if she was trying desperately to hide how much she wanted to know the answer. And if he'd still been unsure if she felt any of what he felt, he got his answer.

And there went any chance of compartmentalisation.

"I'm not," he said, holding her gaze. "Currently. Seeing anyone. You?"

Her throat worked. "This isn't about me."

Ted leaned forward, his forearms on the table. "Adelaid."

Hot pink flushes rising in her cheeks, she still

held his gaze as she said, "I'm not. Seeing anyone. Currently."

"Good," he said. Then, belatedly, added, "That wasn't so hard, was it?"

The pencil went back to tapping against the table—*tap-tap, tappity-tap*—before she said, "Don't think you're off the hook. We've still not found your warm and fuzzies. What did you want to be when you grew up?"

"A scientist. Not the kind that crosses chickens and goats, just a regular, run of the mill scientist."

"Well, that's nice," she said. "As family folklore goes, I wanted to be a tractor."

"Writing came later?"

"Writing came later." She laughed. "Thankfully. For I'm far better at writing than tractoring. I bet you're feeling really glad about that right now."

Infinitely, Ted admitted to himself. Turns out he was infinitely glad.

It was just on dusk when Adelaid left her day shift at the bar.

Her weekly alarm went off, reminding her to drizzle some water on her pet cactus—Spikesaurus Rex. She shot off a quick text to her housemate and best friend, Georgette, reminding her to water her own cactus—Rick the Prick—as well, for he never looked quite as juicy and loved as Rex.

Glancing up as she walked to the tram, so

as not to walk into traffic, Adelaid checked her emails, to find her very first response to her on-spec pitch.

Her heart rocketed when she saw it was from her old employer, who had fingers in all kinds of publishing pies, only it was not from her wonderful editor, Deborah. Some assistant responded and it was a polite, but firm, "Thank you for submitting but it is not what we are currently publishing."

Adelaid's heart blew a gasket and sputtered slowly back to earth.

Disappointing, yes. But not entirely unexpected. There were plenty more fish in the sea.

Her phone rang right as she slipped it back into her backpack.

Ted! Realising her enthusiasm at seeing his name had less to do with the piece, and more to do with the man himself, she frowned.

Yes, he was lovely and polite and kind, yes, he was so gorgeous she felt like her bones were made of butter any time he was near, and yes, she liked the way he looked at her, as if everything she did was pure delight, but it would be very silly to take any of it personally.

So, she cleared her throat and found her professional voice, before answering.

"Ted, hi." Was she late? She sniffed at the argyle vest she wore over a men's button-down. Only a slight scent of beer. "I'm on my way. Promise."

When he spoke the sound broke up, but she thought she heard, "...have to postpone."

"Where are you?" she asked, pressing her ear-bud to her ear as she tried to pick out the background sounds.

"Helipad atop Big Think."

"Right." She had a money tin in which she saved all her coins to pay her electricity bills. Ted had a helipad.

"Last minute trip," he said, his voice thin but sounding as if he as shouting, "in the hopes of buying a business that makes medical supplies. Ronan seems to think if I flap my cape and jiggle my glasses, the stockholders will...how did you put it?"

"Swoon themselves into a stupor?"

"That's the one. Anyway, I'm sorry we have to postpone."

"It's okay," she said, and was surprised to find she actually meant it. She'd been given the brush-off enough times to know this wasn't that.

If she'd been in any doubt at all, it fled when Ted shouted, "Don't hang up. I have a minute."

"How about you call me when you get back?"

"Talk to me now," he said, his voice clearer, as if he'd tucked himself out of the way of the whipping wind.

She looked around, found a bench to sit on. Then reached into her tote for a random pencil and notebook. "Okay. We'll make it a quickie."

"If that's your preference," he said, in that deep husky Ted voice that slid through her like a hot knife through butter.

"Not usually, but needs must." Adelaid bit her lip. They skirted the edges of flirtation every time they met. Apparently, all they needed were phones in hand and the walls came tumbling down.

"Okay, Mr Interviewee, lightning round. Here goes. Ah, what are you reading?"

"Audiobook, *Rivers of London* series. Kindle, *Lincoln in the Bardo*. I don't have as much time to read as I wish. You?"

"Biographies." Adelaid grimaced when she remembered she was meant to remind him that this was her, Adelaid, getting to know him, Ted. Not the other way around. "Religion. Into it?"

"Organised, no. Curiosity as to the why and wherefore? Lifetime hobby. You?"

"Not about me. Sport?"

"Total pro, at watching."

She thought of the way his clothes clung to him, the peaks and valleys of what appeared to be a very well looked after specimen of manhood. A vision of him dripping sweat, in baggy shorts, boxing gloves and nothing else leapt unbidden into her head. A chunk of his dark auburn hair falling over his eyes. Jaw tight. Skin gleaming…

"Adelaid?"

"Sorry. Pets?"

"No."

"Not even a goldfish?"

"Not home enough to take care of one. You?"

She didn't even bother reminding him that time. "What about a plant?"

"You'll find plants are not pets."

"Agree to disagree. So, no plants? Not even a cactus? They're famously low maintenance." A little prickly on the outside, but flourished with the slightest amount of care. Cacti were her people.

"No," said Ted. "Wouldn't be fair."

Fair. To a cactus. Adelaid bit back her sigh.

Then, in case he heard it, she said, "Now this might be several years spent working for a female-centric online social media site talking, but are you by any chance a commitment-phobe?"

He laughed. Then paused. Long enough some deep, soft, shadowy part of herself began to ache.

"No," he said. "In fact, I'm extremely committed. To my work."

"Work schmerk. Haven't you ever come close to...cactus ownership?" She'd nearly said, *Falling in love, settling down, having a half-dozen beautiful, clever, polite babies.*

Something in the way he said, "I have not," had her thinking he'd understood the metaphor just fine.

"But why?" She knew that if he were sitting across a table from her there was no way she'd be so bold. Yet, with the afternoon sun creating great swathes of golden light between the city buildings, and the soft sensuous waft of the evening breeze tickling at her ankles, she felt a little brave, and maybe a little rash. "Have you been unlucky in love?"

A beat, then, "I wouldn't say that."

"Burnt by love?"

"No burns. No scars. My time is simply too precious to have made unjustified choices when it has come to…cacti."

Yeah, he got the metaphor just fine.

"Right, right. So, reading between the lines, it's your fault."

"Excuse me?"

"You have some terrible secret flaw."

"Such as?" he asked, a touch of laughter giving his voice that edge that cut through all her defences every time. Leaving her feeling awfully vulnerable. As if all her cactussy prickles had been plucked away leaving her completely exposed.

"Do you snore, really badly? Or listen to hardcore rap? Or have…a raging case of herpes?"

Definite laughter that time. She could even picture him running a hand up the back of his neck. A thing he did when abashed. It was rather adorable. He was rather adorable, for a huge, hulking, genius billionaire who was the subject of the most important interview of her life so far, and nothing more.

Adelaid prepared to put their phone chat to bed,

when Ted said, "My life goals simply do not run in that direction."

"Herpes?"

"Family."

"I have…no idea how to respond to that."

How could a person's life goals not run to family? She'd adored her mum, despite her mum's best efforts to not always be so adorable. And for all that her brothers drove her bonkers with their overprotection, they'd been the one constant in her life. The ones who loved her, always, despite her nuances.

If her career goal was to be a "highly respected, sartorially envied writer of warm, witty, winning profiles that stun readers with their erudite observations, empathy and heart," her life goals were far more basic.

Security, shelter, family.

"Oh, I doubt that," said Ted.

To which Adelaid blurted, "You can't mean that. Just because you're focussed on work now doesn't mean it has to be your sole focus. And if any genetic material needs to continue on, it's yours. You are doing my entire sex a disservice taking yourself off the market that way!"

Adelaid bit her lip. Clearly, she was the one in need of a safe word.

"Actually," she said, "strike that."

"Which part?" he asked, his voice so deep she

felt it rather than heard it. "The bit about my genetic material or the bit about your sex?"

Adelaid scrunched her eyes shut tight. "I think we've covered that subject to my satisfaction." Not even close, but it was too damn bad. "Let's move on. Favourite colour?"

She felt his pause, felt how far things had suddenly shifted. If her first rule of journalism was to keep herself out of the story, the second was to stay in charge.

"Favourite colour?" she repeated, her voice clipped. No nonsense.

"Green," he said.

"Favourite song?"

"Adelaid," he crooned.

At the tone of his voice, the intimacy, her tenuous hold on tact snapped and she said, "Well, it's either that or I ask *why* you don't imagine yourself having a family. Don't you want kids?"

"No."

"Back to the one-word answers, I see." And not even a second's hesitation.

There was now no stopping the thread of disappointment tying itself in knots in her belly. No denying the fact that while she'd tried to pretend her shock was on behalf of the entire human race, it felt awfully, terribly, dangerously *personal*.

Which was crazy! There was nothing going on between them. Nothing to warrant such a feeling. And yet the ache…it felt all too real.

"Do you not *like* kids?" she asked, a dog with a bone.

"Sawyer's sisters have a bunch. Noisy, sticky, hilarious. Ratbags, but good fun. Harking back to previous points, my commitment is to my work. So, it wouldn't be—"

"Fair," said Adelaid.

"Hmm," he said. Then, "My ride's here. I have to go."

Yes, she thought, *go*. "Thanks for squeezing in a lightning round. I'll use the extra time to really hone my next questions. Sharpen them till they're super-pointy."

"That wasn't pointy?" he asked, his voice rising, the wind once again whipping from his phone to her ears, so that she had to hold the phone away from her ear.

"Ha. Yeah. Maybe a little."

Then the sound became too much, his voice too broken, and as she tried to pick out his words, somewhere in the back of her head she thought he said, "—miss you!"

Which was how Adelaid found herself shouting, "I'll miss you too!"

Before she yanked the phone away from her ear, and jabbed at the red button to hang up the call.

She'd miss him? What on earth was that?

Looking around, reminding herself where she was, she found an old man sitting at the other end of the bench watching as their tram pulled up before them.

He gave her a smile. "Ah, young love."

She opened her mouth to tell the stranger that he had it wrong. That it was nothing like that. Except, the truth of it was, the lines felt a little fuzzy.

Not good. Not good at all. Considering how much she had riding on this.

In the end she gave the stranger a smile. Before hefting her bags higher on her shoulder, jumping on the next tram and heading home.

Ted sat in the bland white room on the fifth floor of Big Think, staring at the empty space where the coffee machine had been.

After the last interview, he'd asked Hadley to strip back even further. Even so far as making the room uncomfortable. And she hadn't disappointed. The blinds had been drawn, the chairs had been swapped out for recycled plastic and the temperature had been turned down to a wintry chill.

Only now—after little more than power-napping for three days straight, needing to liaise constantly via video with the team in Lisbon, who'd had a major breakthrough in a malaria tablet they'd been working on for several years—he could have done with a coffee.

He was so damned spent he hadn't even bothered to come up with a new plan as to how to cope with seeing Adelaid. Maybe that was the answer. Mental and physical exhaustion. When the hairs on the back of his neck tickled, he glanced over his shoulder to see why.

Adelaid Adams stood in the doorway, her hand lifted ready to knock.

Swathed in rich, touchable black velvet that slashed across her decolletage, pinched at her waist and hugged her all the way to her knees, along with a pair of sharp black heels, she looked like she'd stepped straight out of *Mad Men*.

Five days. It had been five days since he'd seen her. Five days spent reliving the moment he'd thought he'd heard her call, "I'll miss you!"

After a week of inhuman hours and intense pressure, that face, those eyes, the frenetic electric energy she carried with her wherever she went, made him feel punch-drunk.

"You okay?" Adelaid asked, not quite meeting his eye as she entered the room and set herself up, tipping her papers and pens and earbuds and phone into the table till the bland room instantly filled with colour and life. "You look a little rough."

Ted could only laugh, considering he'd just been thinking how delectably fresh she looked. "Big week."

Adelaid smoothed her skirt beneath her and sat, before her eyes swung to his. She frowned. Then she reached into her array of bags and pulled out a bag of lollies for herself, and a larger plastic container which she popped open and slid to him.

"Eat," she commanded.

He looked inside and saw a muffin. An actual muffin. Huge, sprinkled in sugar, filled with juicy blueberries. It smelled like warmth, and comfort, and home, the mix creating an unexpected ache deep in his belly that he knew had nothing to do with hunger.

Misreading his silence Adelaid said, "It's home-made."

"By you?"

"Yes," she said, shuffling her papers officiously.

"For me?"

She shot him a look. But didn't deny it. Then fussed with getting her phone recorder set up as she said, "I've seen how much more relaxed you are when fed. When you are relaxed you are more verbal. I've been warming you up till now. This is where we start to get sharp and pointy, remember?"

He remembered. Remembered talking about cacti and goldfish. About partners and children. He also remembered how verbal she'd been when he'd intimated such things were so low on his list of life's priorities they'd fallen off. How inordinately disappointed.

He reminded himself not to let his mother

within ten feet of her, as they'd have plenty to talk about.

Ted tore a chunk from the top of the muffin. When it hit his tongue his brain all but whimpered in relief at the hit of sugar, and fruit and warmth.

Burning the midnight oil and eating when it occurred to him might have suited when he was nineteen, but he truly needed to look after himself better. If he collapsed, he'd be no use to anyone. And yet while his life was dedicated to taking care of others, this was the first time in as long as he could remember that someone other than his inner circle had gone out of their way to take care of him.

"Shall we?" she said.

"Hit me."

"Tell me about your family."

Ted coughed on the muffin. Adelaid noticed. But she did not back down. In fact, there was a newfound determination in her today. Back straight, fidgets minimal. He wondered why.

She didn't give him the chance to ponder, saying, "Let's start with your mum."

Leaving Ted to remind himself that this was their relationship. She the interviewer, he the interviewee. His mission to help create a new narrative for the company, to build trust with new investors, to show them why Big Think deserved their benefaction above all other options.

So he began. "My mother, Celia. Imagine a small, neat, red-headed whirling dervish always off volunteering or taking classes. Stubborn, adoring, brilliant, wise. I—"

"You?"

"Ought to give her a call."

At that, she softened, just a smidge. "Yes, you ought. And your dad?"

Ted had been waiting for this one. His origin story was branded into Big Think legend: his father's sudden illness, how it had sparked his determination to turn his talents to curing the world's great ills. He had a stock answer to such a question that he had been using for years—three lines total, ready and prepared.

Only this time he had the taste of berries and sugar on his tongue. And a woman in the pursuit of…how had she put it? Connection and empathy.

He looked to his father's watch, ran his thumb over the face and said, "I was nineteen when my father died. It was unexpected. Devastating, in fact."

The stern comportment flickered. Her voice, when it came, gentle, yet unyielding. "How?"

"Cancer."

"What kind?"

He lifted his eyes to hers. "Pancreatic."

She nodded, her eyes clear. No pity, no sorrow. Her expression measured. As if she understood trauma. As if she'd been honed by it herself.

"I was away," said Ted, "when he fell ill. On a gap year part way through uni. Three days after his diagnosis, he was gone."

"Do you mean… Did you get home in time? To see him before he passed?"

Ted shook his head. "I tried. But we didn't know it would be that fast. There were no signs, you see. No warning. Or I'd have never…"

Ted shifted in the small hard plastic seat, cursing himself for thinking it would make a lick of difference. "Looking back there was weight loss, lack of appetite. Ironically, they were on a health kick. Turned out he was suffering terrible pain for some time but did not want to worry Mum, as they were due to meet me overseas for her fiftieth birthday."

"You said it was devastating. What did that look like?"

He glanced to her. Her eyes were huge, brimming with empathy. But still she didn't back down.

"I was angry, for a long time. Guilt-ridden, of course. But also filled with a river of rage. Towards him. Towards my dad, for not letting on." Ted ran a hand over his mouth, elbows now braced against the table. "Once home, I stayed. Moved from straight science into medicine. Hurtled through a five-year degree in three. Wangled my way into concurrent doctorates. As if it might somehow contract time and undo what had happened. Needless to say, I wasn't in my right mind for some time. It was only due to Sawyer, and Ronan, that I stayed out of any real trouble, as I was looking for it all the same."

Movement dragged Ted from his memories, and he looked up to find Adelaid had her elbows on the table now too. Her chin on her palm, her expression gripped. He'd surprised her, proving himself not quite the good guy she'd built him up to be. And yet, she wasn't fazed. Quite the opposite. Something in her eyes willed him on. Green fire that shone from within.

"Does that make me sound cold?" he asked her, voicing something he'd long since wondered but never said out loud, not to Ronan, or Sawyer, or even to himself. "Does it make me a cold-hearted bastard wishing he'd lived longer, not for himself, but for me?"

She shook her head. "It makes you human."

At which point she put down her pencil and went to switch off the recorder on her phone.

Till Ted held out a hand. His reach bringing his fingers near hers. "Don't stop." Ted pulled his hand back to his side of the table and licked a stray crumb from the end of his thumb. "Perhaps there is magic in your muffins, after all."

"No perhaps about it," she said, her gaze caught on his mouth, darkening when his tongue swiped over his bottom lip.

When she drew in a long deep breath, her composure slipping, the energy she'd been containing, on his behalf, now rushing through the room, all but lifting his hair, Ted had to shift again, but for other reasons.

"Was he much like you?" she asked. "You described your mother as small, so I imagine your father must have been quite the opposite."

"In looks, yes. He was a big guy, upright, imposing. In temperament he was more studious. A professor of history. A lot of my childhood was spent reading in our library. My mother, smarter than us both by half, prefers romance novels. Truer than any tale told by old men with a legacy to protect, she likes to say."

Adelaid laughed, the sound intimate, husky. "I like the sound of her, very much."

Ted leant forward, his forearms resting the table as he picked up one of Adelaid's pencils and twirled it back and forth. "She'd like you too, I think."

"You *think*?"

He lifted his eyes to hers. "I know it. In fact, she might like you more than me."

Adelaid blinked. Several times in quick succession. Her cheeks pinking, her mouth kicking up at one corner. "I doubt that."

"Ah, but I'm busy. And don't make time. While I feel as if you would be the opposite. That you dote on your family."

"Don't be so sure." Then, noting her relapse,

she sat up tall. Notched her shoulders back and asked, "Siblings?"

He shook his head.

"So you're an only child. Do you think *that's* part of your reason for not imagining yourself with a family?" she asked, her eyes suddenly intense. "Because I'm from a big family and can't imagine anything else."

"I'm not sure I understand…"

Her mouth popped open before she snapped it shut. Then she shook her head and said, "Sorry, um, I mean… Your parents—was it their dream to have a small tight family, such as it was?"

"Ah, no," he said. "I think my mother would have loved a big family, but there were complications, after I was born. My mother jokes about it, says I broke the mould. But my dad always…" He paused. "My father used to look so stricken whenever it came up, so I imagine it must have been fraught. He adored her, you see. They adored one another. Very much."

Watching his mother grieve had been untenable. His own guilt and rage and sorrow nothing compared to hers. He knew then that he could never put himself in such a position. Especially since using his gifts to stop others from feeling such pain was a more noble pursuit.

A scraping sound reached Ted's ears, before the small container of snake lollies appeared under his nose. "In my experience, sugar always helps."

Ted laughed. And took a few.

"You should know how nice it is, hearing you talk about your parents that way. Fondly. With such acceptance." Adelaid's hand stayed near the container, fingers curled towards her palm. "And in case I didn't make it clear, you can call blueberry muffin at any time. Even retroactively."

"It's okay," he said, feeling light-headed, and not from the sugar. As if he'd loosened his grip on things he'd been holding too tight for too long. "Do with it what you will."

"Thank you." With that she pulled her hand back, collected her phone and pressed the button to end the recording.

Only she didn't make to leave.

And neither did he. "You mentioned brothers. Are you close with your family?"

"Ah. Too close, one might say." A shrug. "They are all a fair bit older than me, and a long time ago took it upon themselves to keep a close eye."

"Did you need a close eye?"

Her mouth twisted. "At one time. My childhood was a little less stable than yours. No reading in the library, that's for sure. My mum had my oldest brother Brad when she was really young, and was never quite able to make a go of things from there. We each had different fathers. Not a one of them stuck around."

Unlike Ted's dad, who he'd loved so much he

was still trying to save him more than a decade after his death.

"And my mum… She died when I was really young."

"Sorry to hear that."

A quick smile. A learned response. "I don't remember as much as I would like. Flashes I'm not even sure are even real. Are they based on photos? Or stories my brothers have told? I wish I could be sure."

"It terrified me," Ted admitted, "how soon I began to forget my dad. The sound of his voice, the timbre of his laugh. After the blur of the early days of his loss, I took the time to talk to his students, his colleagues, his friends. I researched memory tricks. I started wearing his watch, all so I could feel close to him again."

Ted slipped the watch off his wrist and looked at the face.

"May I?" Adelaid asked.

He handed it to her, watched as she felt the weight of it in her hand.

When she ran the pad of her thumb over the face of the watch, the exact way he himself did a dozen times a day, something yanked hard in Ted's belly. And he felt himself unspool, completely. Such that he might never be put back together quite the same way again.

She passed the watch back, and he slid it

straight back onto his wrist, looking to tap into some place solid, and familiar.

"I do what I do because of him. Big Think exists because of him. We do what we do here so that less and less families will suffer as mine did."

If I stop, Ted thought, *stop working, stop pushing, stop focussing, stop working through the night if that's what it takes, then who am I?*

"Thank goodness for you," Adelaid said with a sigh. "Because suffering sucks."

"Did cancer take your mum too?"

"Ah, no. She fell. Slipped on the driveway. Hit her head. I was home from school that day. Home from school a lot of days actually as time management was not her strong suit. I was the one who found her."

Ted ran his hand over his face, before he let it drop to the table, near hers. A small gesture of solidarity.

"She drank, you see. A lot. Looking back there was likely some underlying factor, bipolar, perhaps? But she was never diagnosed. Would never have occurred to her to try. Despite that, or maybe because of it, she was really special, my mum. My brothers, being older, remember things a little differently, but to me she was this funny, bright, shiny, wonderful creature. And she adored us. So so much."

She lifted her hand in a shrug before letting it

drop to the table, face up, now mere millimetres from his own.

Before he could think about it, Ted tipped his thumb so that it stroked along the side of her hand. Her fingers curled towards her palm, as if the nerves had been switched on by his touch, and his insides responded in kind. Tightening. Tensing. Readying.

Then slowly, slowly, she turned her hand, tipping it into his. An exploration. Then a tangling as their fingers moved over one another, hooking and touching and—

Adelaid withdrew her hand with an indrawn breath, tucking it under the table, out of sight.

But it was too late. The moment had happened. Attraction, magnetism, compulsion, chemistry, biology, physics. All were at play here—within her as they were within him.

Her energy crackling now, spilling out of her till it filled the room, Adelaid's eyes were wide and bright as they connected with his.

"It might not have been bipolar," she said. "Might have been ADHD. It tends to run in families. And I have it. I have ADHD."

Her face came over a little pale as she dropped the news. Her body braced, for...what? For him to wince, or scoff, or gasp in shock?

It wasn't shocking to him in the slightest. He'd had some idea that might be the case. The circles he ran in, neurodiversity was essential. Imperative to finding new angles from which to attack the kinds of problems he was determined to solve.

His only concern was the way she'd told him, like she was dropping a little bomb. And why she'd chosen that moment to do so. Right on the back of a level of intimacy that still had him reeling.

Adelaid was testing him. To what end?

His mind sifted briskly through research he'd read, and conversations broached over the years with colleagues with ADHD—both impulsive and inattentive, figuring Adelaid likely the latter.

"Day dreamer?" he said, keeping his face neutral.

She jerked, gaze wary, but at least colour crept back into her cheeks. "For sure."

He motioned to the now empty muffin container. "You prefer baking to standing over a stove?"

"I do. I get too distracted. It's not safe. I set fire to the microwave once, defrosting a piece of bread." Her eyes glinted as she tossed more and more grenades. "Typed in twenty minutes rather than twenty seconds, drifted into the room next door and forgot about it. My housemate, Georgette, who was in the shower, alerted me to the fact the house smelled funny."

Ted nodded. Avoiding looking at her scattered notes, the pages covered in question marks and balloons, and remembered when he'd called it *pure chaos*.

The flash in her eyes that day hadn't been fighting spirit. It had been hurt. Because to her it wasn't chaos; it was the opposite. It was determined organisation of scattered thought. It was a pathway through.

And, it seemed, he was not the first to call attention to it in a way that made her feel bad.

Wishing he could go back, and handle himself better, show her that he didn't find her ways confronting, that he thought her an absolute delight, he instead smiled into her eyes.

"I had to learn ways," he said, "to manage my rage. To manage my grief. To not give in to it, but to *harness* it. I expect you've learned to do the same."

Her eyes flicked to his. As if she couldn't quite believe how this conversation had gone. Should she keep fighting him or talk to him? Give him some insight into her life for a time.

"Calendars," she said, stopping to lick her lips, "timers. Music helps, the white noise in my ears helps me concentrate. As does pen on paper, doodling. Change of scene if I can't stay on task. And being around people who get it, who roll with it rather than finding it frustrating. That helps. Though it's been by far the hardest part."

He understood that. All too well. Knew how lucky he was to have had Sawyer and Ronan.

"And where do you fall down?" he asked.

She laughed, though there was no humour in it. "You say that as if it's totally okay to fail."

"Isn't it? I fail all the time. Constantly. Science is ninety-nine percent failure. But without knowing what's not true, how will we ever find out what is?"

He watched her as she took that on. As she let it slide into her psyche. As she let it change her. This open-hearted, open-minded, gladly evolving creature of light and wonder and—

"I can be a little tactless. At times. And I internalise," she said, her gaze no longer avoiding his. In fact, she seemed more than happy to keep her eyes on him. "A lot. I'm not very good at asking for help. Probably because my brothers have been determined to give it to me whether I need it or not."

Then, after nibbling at the inside of her cheek, she said, "I'm pretty good at impulse control except when it comes to vintage clothes. I'm hypersensitive to certain fabrics, but I can't resist anything that looks like it might once have been on a fifties movie set. My mum and I loved watching those old movies together. The women were so beautiful. And so bad-ass."

Ted laughed. And earned himself the sweetest smile, pure sunshine.

Then she asked, "How about you? Where do you fall down? Personally, I mean, not with the science. Or is that a silly question? You're so successful, and have more money than any one person ought. Your best friends are your work partners, and you sound more like brothers than colleagues. Despite needing to call your mother, I'm certain she's beyond chuffed to have you as her son."

Ted could see how she thought all of that, but every brick she laid on the pedestal she built wobbled at least a little.

When had he last had a drink with his friends? When had he last celebrated a breakthrough, rather than swiftly moving onto the next? When had he last made actual dedicated time for a woman? When had he last slept? He wondered how well he'd been coping, after all.

He ran a hand up the back of his neck. "I fear you've built far too generous a picture of me; your readers will hardly believe it's true. Give it time and I'm sure you'll uncover enough flaws to balance it out." Then, "How about we call time on today?"

"Yes!" she said, sitting up tall. "Of course."

Then she swept her gear into her bags, heaved them over her shoulder and followed Ted out of the room. Where they walked down the empty hall, side by side.

When they reached the lifts, Ted asked, "When can I see you again?"

Her eyes sparked, then dimmed. "For the next interview. Um, I'll text you?"

"Okay."

Her lift opened first and she stepped inside. "Till then."

"Till then," said Ted, watching her till the doors closed.

And when they did, he breathed out hard. Alone in the darkening hallways as the sensor lights dimmed, as if she'd taken the light with her.

He swiped his card over the sensor, readying to head back to his lair. Back to the email lemmings, and the malaria tablets.

Only something stopped him. Some new flicker of sense. The knowledge it might actually serve him better to ease off the accelerator on occasion. To sleep, to eat, to call his mother.

Inside the lift he pressed the button for the lobby.

And once outside he breathed in fresh air. Smiled at strangers. And if he checked each tree he passed, just in case a kitten might need a little hand from a tall guy with a little unexpected time on hands, then so be it.

CHAPTER FOUR

ADELAID SHUFFLED UNSEEINGLY through the rack of vintage dresses.

She usually found the op shop scent of camphor and the scratchy feel of old wool a comfort. But her mind was all over the place.

Except it wasn't all over the place. It was in one place. Replaying the joy on Ted's face when she gave him the muffin. The ache in his kind brown eyes when he'd spoken about his dad. The absolute ease with which he took the news of her ADHD. The way he'd held her hand.

Or had she held his? In the end it had been mutual, that much she did know. Fingers slipping over one another, slowly, intimately, searchingly. It had been one of the single most sensual moments of her entire life.

She'd never played footsies or handsies with an interview subject before. In fact, the very thought was utterly laughable! No, not laughable. Wrong. Very, *very* wrong.

So why had it felt so utterly, so absolutely, so heartachingly, right?

"Addy!"

Adelaid flinched, before turning to find Georgette hustling into the op shop. "Hey."

"Find anything good?" Georgette grabbed a felt fedora with musketeer feather off a mannequin's head before putting it on her own and heading to a table covered in concert T-shirts.

Adelaid checked the price tag on a silk shirt before putting it straight back on the rack. Working three part-time jobs—writing small pieces for community papers, working the occasional shift as a bartender in a city dive bar and a little dog-walking—while taking her shot, rather than one time-sucking job that paid rather a lot more, meant she had to be careful with her money right now.

"Plenty. But my cupboards are full."

She headed over to help Georgette look through the stacks for a Guns N' Roses shirt she'd been searching for for months, then they were heading to a local café. They had a shared home office in their rental around the corner, but a change of view was one of the best ways Adelaid had learned to stay on task.

Unlike work colleagues she knew who could only write with quiet and a shut door, she could work from home, in cafés, in parks, on trains, at a rock concert. A true benefit of her condition. And it *did* have benefits. Ted was right about that.

And there she was, thinking about Ted again.

Yes, she was easily distracted. Yes, she never remembered where she'd left her keys. Yes, she struggled with time management. Yes, she could be quick-tempered. But she loved that she was a dreamer. It was one of her favourite things about herself. She lived for the great bursts of creativity, the endless energy, the wells of enthusiasm. If she found something engaging, if she spent time doing the things that brought her joy, her hyperfocus made her unstoppable.

When he'd asked how she'd learned to "harness" her condition, as if that was a perfectly normal question, she could have kissed him. Literally climbed over the desk, taken his beautiful face in hand and kissed his beautiful mouth.

Again, *wrong*. Which was how she'd managed to contain herself. Just.

Except no one, not a GP, not a counsellor, not anyone in any online groups she dipped in an out of, had ever put it that way.

As for her brothers? Sheesh! They *still* couldn't commend her for how she managed her condition. They only saw the times she lost time, or was a little tactless, or zoned out mid-conversation as proof that she wasn't "getting better."

When it was normal to slip.

Getting back up again was the important part.

"Your brothers called," said Georgette, right on cue.

Of course they did. "Which ones?"

"Sid. Brad. Invite to a kindy music event for some nephew or another. Asking if you need money. Checking to see if you're alive. The usual."

Adelaid shoved her hands into the pockets of her second-hand overalls, and managed not to roll her eyes so far they hurt. For something else that had come out of her conversation with Ted was some new insight into why her brothers acted the way they did.

Being so much older, they'd no doubt seen far more of their mum's erratic behaviour. That must have been pretty frightening at times. Surely it had impacted them in ways she'd not been privy to. That, then losing their mum, and taking on responsibility for an eight-year-old girl, it couldn't have been easy.

She so desperately wanted them to give her some grace, but there might be room for her to do the same for them.

"I'll call them back later. Shall we?" Adelaid asked.

Georgette put the hat back on the mannequin and followed her out of the op shop and up the road to the café. Where they plonked themselves at the tall bench by the window and set themselves up for the morning.

"How's your thing going?" Georgette asked as she perused the menu.

"It goes…fine." Adelaid opened the so-far-blank Word file on her computer.

"Just fine?" Georgette nudged, for she had skin in the game, having given Adelaid an in with the PR firm she worked for.

"I meant amazing," said Adelaid, wafting a hand over her notebooks. "So amazing you will bathe in the reflected glory of my glowing words, for the story will be amazing. Because Ted is amazing. And, as you well know, I am—"

"Amazing?"

"Exactly." Adelaid batted her lashes at her friend before looking back at the blank screen. Then she blurted, "I told him I have ADHD."

"Oh, wow." Georgette had been around long enough to know how that usually went down. "Were you okay? Were you having an episode?"

"I was fine! I am fine. I just…told him." To be true, she'd kind of thrown it at him in a fit of panic. Not one of her proudest moments.

"And how did he react?"

"With aplomb. Did I mention he's kind of amazing?"

"Huh. I saw him the other day, when I was given a magical golden ticket into the Big Think building to pitch some social media stuff. Two of them—your Ted and Ronan Gerard—walked through the lobby and you could feel the oestro-

ALLY BLAKE

97

gen levels rising. All loping alpha strides, full-
on Disney prince hair and those shoulders. Why
didn't you tell me how gorgeous he was when
you pitched the story?"

"I didn't know how gorgeous he was then."

"Fair enough. Just tell me this—what does he
look like without the glasses? Has he spilled some
scientific experiment on himself mid-interview
and had to change, in front of you, from one hot
button-down shirt into another?"

Adelaid gave Georgette a look. "You know I
can't talk about what I'm writing while I'm writing it."

Georgette sighed. "Your muse is so bloody precious."

He really was. But that wasn't why she'd yet
to write an actual word about Ted Fincher in an
actual Word file.

In her old job she'd been trained to write suc-
cinctly, to write with a clear intention and to write
fast. She worked like a machine.

But there was also a healthy kind of disconnect. A sense of hovering above, writing from a
bird's-eye view, that kept her focus entirely on
the subject. She took care not to impose any of
herself on her writing, other than natural empathy that it was her mission to impart.

Ted asked her about her life all the time. About
her family, her foibles, her vulnerabilities, her
hopes, the things that made her happy. While

she, for some reason, couldn't seem to get past the fact that he didn't imagine himself having a family of his own.

Disconnect wasn't possible when Ted held open doors for her, and made her coffee, and ate the food she'd baked for him. When he looked at her the way he did, and listened to her the way he did, and saw her the way he did, and touched her the way he did.

It was hard. And getting harder to keep things… separate.

But what choice did she have?

She set up a pomodoro timer on her phone, popped her earbuds in her ears and placed her fingers over the keys.

She had plenty to work with now—his college days with Ronan and Sawyer, stories of his good works. And now she had the puzzle piece that always brought a story together, that gave it gravitas, that would spark empathy in the reader.

She had the why. His father. He'd done all that he'd done, built an empire, in fact, because he hadn't been able to save his dad.

Feelings swelling inside of her as she remembered the way he'd looked at her when she'd held his father's watch, she placed her fingers over the keys and—

Her phone pinged.

Ted. Was he thinking of her, thinking of when

their hands had touched? Thinking of what it might have felt like if they hadn't stopped there?

She reached for her phone so fast she nearly knocked it to the floor. Only to find the Adams family chat.

Brad: Sunday dinner. My place. Be there.

She put her phone down, only for it to ping again.

Brad: Addy? Knock-knock?

Adelaid: Can't. Working.

Brad: Take a break.

Adelaid: Don't want to.

Brad: Don't want to, or boss won't let you. Need me to have a word?

Just like that all the love and understanding she'd been feeling for her brothers went up in smoke.

Adelaid: As I have told you, on many occasions, I am a grown-up person who is fully able to fight my own battles. Make my own decisions. I'll come see you all soon. When I can. Promise.

She turned her phone to silent.

The sooner she had her interview done, and written, and in the marketplace, the sooner she had a fancy by-line and a nice cheque and her next big story lined up, the better.

When her phone buzzed again, she ignored it.

Let her mind go to Ted, to his warm eyes, and his deep voice, and his kindness, then made herself focus on his conviction. To big traumas, that led to big dreams.

To the story she could tell.

And she began to type.

Ted's phone rang as he was pounding the indoor running track built into the private gym a couple of floors below his lair.

He tapped the button on his earbuds to take the call, his voice hoarse as he said, "Fincher."

"Darling!"

"Mum?" Ted slowed to a jog.

"Of course it's me. Unless someone else in your life calls you darling. Though I wouldn't put it past Sawyer. Such a cheeky boy."

Her ears must have been burning. His last chat with Adelaid had forced him to admit he'd been slack when it came to checking in of late. They had a weekly call every Friday at five, but apart from that he'd not found the time to call more for a while now.

About the time she'd started nudging him about

his quality of life. Which, she'd begun to intimate, meant more to her than his work ever would.

But she was his only family, and he hers. He needed to do better.

On that, it was neither five nor a Friday, meaning she was the one calling out of time.

"What's wrong?" he asked, breaths coming harder as he paced to grab a towel from the bench by the double-glazed windows looking out over the Melbourne CBD. Even without his glasses he could see the rain pelting down outside, coating the glass in tracks of steely grey.

"Wrong? Why does something have to be wrong?"

When he heard the clatter of cutlery and laughter in the background, the sounds of a busy café rather than a busy hospital, his heart ceased to rattle inside his chest.

His mother's voice softened, as if it had occurred to her that, belatedly, considering their history, his question had weight. "I'm fine, darling. I just miss the sound of your voice. Hang on a second."

The phone muffled as if his mother had pressed a hand over the microphone, though he could still hear her shout, "Proper milk, cream on top and chocolate powder. No sugar!" before she came back with, "Now, where were we?"

Ted wrapped his towel around his neck and

stretched out his shoulders. "You missed the sound of my voice."

"Right. So tell me, what's new with you?"

"Promising outcomes in the treatment of throat cancers from the Singapore lab."

"That's nice." A pause, then, "Though I was hoping you might have been up to something on a more…personal front."

And this was usually where things started to get tense. Celia pressing forward, Ted retreating. Only this time, before he had the chance to duck and weave, Adelaid Adams slipped into his mind. Her smile, her bright eyes, her chin resting on her palm when she forgot she was meant to be taking notes, and simply listened as he spoke.

Then there was that husky intake of breath when he'd stroked her hand with his thumb. That had played out on repeat in his mind for days.

"Nothing to speak of," he croaked, then cleared his throat.

"Hmm. And yet a little bird told me you have been spending time with a lovely young woman."

Ted dropped the towel onto his head. "What little bird might that be?"

Ronan? Surely not. Hadley, then. For she enjoyed nothing more than watching Ted, Sawyer and Ronan squirm.

"Someone who adores you," his mother chastised. "And like me believes you need to be thinking of yourself more. You're not getting any younger, my love. And I'd hate for you to wake up one day and realise how much time you've wasted—"

"Mum. I am not wasting my time." Quite the opposite. He had used every second he had.

"Of course not, darling. Now tell me about her. Is she kind? Funny? Smart? Of course she is. Or she'd not have caught your attention. Is she pretty? Not that it matters. What's her name?"

As Celia kept chattering on, asking all sorts of questions, from the ridiculous to the sublime, Ted grabbed his father's watch from the bench and placed it over his wrist. Swiping his thumb over the face. Checking in.

Only this time he didn't simply see his father's kindly face. He saw him rolling his eyes at his mother's chatter. Before those same eyes swam with adoration for the woman he'd married. As if he couldn't believe his luck that a quiet, studious nerd such as himself had landed such a woman. Had been gifted such a family.

Ted sucked in a breath. His fist pressing against his ribs.

That might have been his father's dream, but it wasn't his.

Maybe, a voice popped up in the back of his head, *maybe it might have been. It would have been likely, in fact, if circumstance hadn't ripped your family apart.*

But it had been ripped apart. Broken. Missing a

piece so that it could never be whole again. There was no getting around that. No getting over it. No way would he put himself in a position to go through that again.

When his mum started asking after his "new lady friend" and her medical history, including potential allergies, in case a time came that they ate together, and it was Celia's turn to choose the restaurant, no doubt picturing the two-storey house they could move into, bay windows, big backyard, oak tree with a swing, a library she could help fill, Ted cut her off.

"Mum, Adelaid is a journalist. Writing a story about Big Think. That's why we have been spending time together. That's all."

"Oh. There's really nothing more?"

"Mum."

"Adelaid, you say?"

"With one 'e,'" Ted added, then shook his head.

"That's different. Lovely but different."

A frisson of warmth wavered down his spine, hearing his mother describe Adelaid to a T, without having met her. As if knowing that's exactly the kind of woman he'd spend time with, if it was up to him.

"Well then," she said, "I guess the little bird was wrong. I look forward to reading her article."

"Great." Ted rubbed a hand over his eyes before putting his glasses back on.

"Talk soon. And be good!"

"You too," he said. Then rang off.

Too cool to keep running, despite the energy now coursing through him, energy in need of release, he stretched out his legs to stave off lactic acid itch.

And uncooperative thoughts. Meaning Adelaid Adams.

The time came in any series of experiments when a scientist had to admit defeat. Einstein himself was meant to have said that insanity was doing the same thing over and over again and expecting different results.

Adelaid was under his skin. Rather than expelling so much time and energy into pushing her away, perhaps the time had come to make room for her instead, lest she barrel right through him.

His intention, when committing himself to Big Think for life, had never been all work and no play. Meaning he needed to be elastic enough to allow for a little levity, for some pleasure. So long as it fell within a predetermined margin of error. So long as he remained in control.

He employed thousands, across continents. He was in charge of billions of dollars of funding. He made decisions that meant life-changing research was funded, while others were not. The level of control, of discipline, of focus, that required was astronomical. And he did so without breaking a sweat.

Surely, he could let himself adore Adelaid Adams, if that's what it took to survive her?

Juggling her bags, and a coffee, and the funny little thing she'd picked up for Ted, Adelaid trekked across the Big Think forecourt.

Her head was tight from staying up too late writing. But it had been exactly what she needed. A fire lit under her, reminding her that while she seemed to have developed a little crush on her subject, the purpose of their meetings was for her, Adelaid, to get to know him, Ted. And that was all.

"Adelaid?"

She looked up to find a woman walking her way. Late sixties, neat auburn bob, pleasant. A stranger yet somehow familiar.

"Hi?" Adelaid said.

Hand to heart the woman said, "I'm Celia Fincher. Ted's mum. I adore your outfit. Reminds me of Rosalind Russell in—" Celia clicked her fingers.

"His Girl Friday?"

"That's the one!"

Adelaid couldn't help her smile. The shoulder pads were a bit tricky to navigate especially with her work tote, laptop bag and handbag, but the "newspaper woman" suit was a favourite. And she needed all the help she could get.

She hitched the bags slipping off her shoulder. "Are you here to see Ted? Did I get the time wrong? It happens."

"Not at all. Ted took me out for breakfast, and when he mentioned he was meeting you, well… I may have stretched out our catch-up a little longer." A crafty smile, then, "And what's that you've got there?"

Adelaid followed Celia's line of sight to find the cute little cactus with its tufty pink flower on top sitting high in its bright yellow pot. "It's for Ted."

Celia's eyebrows rose. "It's not his birthday till September."

"It's a bit of an in-joke."

Was it? Or was it that she couldn't let go of the fact that he thought himself not cut out for a family? If she proved that he could keep a cactus alive he might change his mind. Best not share all that with his mother.

"You're itching to ask me about him, aren't you?" Celia said.

"What? No. Of course not." Except… Ted Fincher's mother. Right before her. Clearly keen as mustard to talk about her son.

"What would you like to know?" Celia asked.

Everything. Every moment, every heartache, every joy, every success, every misstep, that made him the man he was today.

Adelaid waved a hand in the air between them.

When it dropped to her bag strap she began to fiddle with the stitching. "I'm fine. Really."

"Are you sure? Ted's never been much of a sharer. Holds it all in. Strong silent type, like his father."

Not with me, Adelaid thought, then bit her lip.

Right then, Ted burst through the rotating glass doors in the distance, glancing at his watch, then running a hand through his thick hair. Clearly not happy that, for once, he was the one who was late.

Then he began to jog. All long loping strides, his hair lifting and falling. Sunlight glinting off his dark-rimmed glasses. Clark Kent through and through.

When he spotted her, a smile broke out across his face. And Adelaid could only hope it wasn't obvious, *to his mother*, that her heart had begun to thump against her ribs at the sight of him. Her *little crush* feeling mighty heavy against her chest.

"Mum?" said Ted, slowing as he neared, his hand landing on his mother's back as he pulled up beside her.

"Ted, darling. Look who I just banged into."

"Right. So you've introduced yourselves, then."

"We've had a lovely chat."

He sent Adelaid a look of deep apology, even going so far as to mouth the word *Sorry!* behind his mother's back.

Adelaid shook her head, infinitesimally, intimating it was just fine. Even while she gripped the cactus pot a little tighter.

"And now we say goodbye, Mum."

"Goodbye, darling," said Celia. She lifted her cheek and he kissed it. "Lovely to meet you, Adelaid. Make sure you show the world how special this one is. He broke the mould."

"So he told me."

"He did? Well, fancy that."

Ted gave his mother a look, then a gentle turn and a gentle shove, which made her laugh, before she waved and left.

Once it was just the two of them, Ted moved closer to Adelaid, hands delving into the pockets of his suit pants as together they watched his mother totter towards a nice-looking town car with a driver ready to whisk her away.

"So that's your mother," said Adelaid.

"Mmm. Any chance you're going to tell me what you were talking about?"

"Toilet training, your favourite cuddle toy, your Superman onesies."

When she looked his way, he was watching her. Watching her with an intensity she'd not seen in him before now. "I never had Superman onesies."

"Really?" She swallowed. "My mistake."

When he kept watching her, his mouth lifting into a smile that said things, meant things, asked for things, she felt her bones start to go all noodly. For, when he chose it, that smile of his was a freaking weapon.

"Here," she said, shoving her gift at him. "This is for you. It's a powder puff."

Ted took the cactus, the pot engulfed by his large hand. "It's a cactus."

"A *pet* cactus," Adelaid corrected.

She saw the moment he got the joke, his eyes crinkling, his cheeks lifting before he burst into laughter, the sound as deep and rich and wonderful as she'd imagined it might be.

"Thank you. I'll take good care of it."

She nodded. "I know you will."

Then, because all the swirly undercurrents of unsaid things began to feel a little heavy, Adelaid started walking towards Big Think, hoping the ground might shore up sometime before she got there.

Till Ted tilted his chin in the opposite direction. "Let's walk a little. I've started having nightmares about that office and its freaky white walls."

"I didn't want to say, but it's not really the most inspiring space."

"That was the point, I'm afraid. I thought it might help us both…stick to the brief."

Adelaid went to ask why he thought they'd needed help, till it hit her. That would be opening up a can of worms they'd not be able to put back.

"Somewhere new this time?"

"Sounds good." His smile was warm, easy, his

comportment looser than usual as he fell into step beside her, cactus balanced on the palm of his hand.

When his eyes found hers again his smile deepened. Made her feel all hot and melty inside.

"So, that was your mother?"

Ted winced. "That was my mother. I blame you for all that back there. After our conversation the other day I felt guilted into taking her out for breakfast."

"Ah. No wonder she was so keen to meet me."

"Oh, I'm certain that's not the half of it," he said, but left it at that.

Adelaid breathed out. Hard. While she'd been busy reminding herself that they were interview subject and interviewer, something quite other had come over Ted. And for the first time since they'd met, she wasn't sure who was in control.

"Either way," Adelaid said, "she raised you well. She must be chuffed to have such a polite son."

He shot her a look, but the watery sunlight glinted off his glasses and she couldn't see his eyes. "Polite."

"You are polite! It's a good thing. I promise. Lovely, really. A lost art. I've met plenty of people who are not nearly as kind, or understanding, or patient, as you."

"What people?"

"It doesn't matter."

"Give me their names."

"I'm not giving you any names." Adelaid laughed up at him, then took his arm as they squeezed up against a building when a widespread tour group went by. When she went to take her hand away, his closed over hers, keeping it there.

Using it to tug her to a halt in the middle of the footpath, turning so he faced her. "I can be grumpy."

"Sure, you can."

"Surly too."

"If you say so."

"If frustrated, tired, hungry, ignored, I can be downright grim."

His touch was light, and yet she felt as if her arm was on fire. So much so she let her bags slide down her arm, and used it as an excuse to move out of range, as she went to loop her bags over the other shoulder.

At least that was her plan, till Ted's long blunt fingers hooked under the straps, and easy as you please he tossed them over his own beefy shoulder.

"I can carry my own bags," she said, feeling flustered now. By the change in him. And meeting his mother. And the fact that he was helping her when she did not need his help. The way her brothers did all the time.

"I'm well aware," he said. "Probably why you walk with a tilt."

She was building up a nice head of steam but

that stopped when she rolled her shoulders, wriggling her hips to see if he might be right.

"Coming," he said, her bags still in place, for they wouldn't dare slip off his shoulder. Oh, no. His gaze determined. Not to be messed with. As if he'd come to some decision, and enough was enough. Add mussed dark hair with those glints of auburn, and crooked glasses, and superhero jaw walking by him, up close and personal, near enough to feel the heat emanating from him, it was quite the thing.

So, she joined him. She'd take her bags back in a bit. Once feeling came back to her arm. "I might do things differently to the way you do them but that does not make me helpless."

"I know."

The thing was, she believed him. While the very last thing she needed in her life was another man thinking she needed looking after, she was tired and he was there, and even while acting all alpha and in charge, he never made her feel dependant.

He made her feel seen.

Unprepared for that revelation, she felt it like a shock of adrenaline to the heart. As if her crush had been given growth hormones, it swelled till she could no longer grapple the thing. No longer keep it under wraps. All she could hope to do was keep Ted distracted so that he had no clue.

"What was your mum's name?" Ted asked.

"Aren't I the one who's meant to be asking the questions?"

"Change of plan," said Ted, his jaw hard, his gaze intent.

"Just like that?"

"Just like that."

Well, if he was asking questions, maybe he wouldn't notice the fact that her pulse was throbbing in her throat, or that her cheeks felt as if they were on fire, or that every time his arm brushed hers, she shivered. Adelaid began to feel hollow inside. As if she could sense the thing that would fill her, only was too afraid to ask.

"Fine!" she said, throwing out her hands. "My mum's name was Vivian."

"Tell me a memory you think is true."

Not sure where he was going with this, she answered, "I think I mentioned she wasn't much into clocks, rules, school. She was a little wild. Made choices that made it harder for herself." A shrug, then, "I think it was easier to sit me down with an old Danny Kaye movie than deal with my behaviour."

Ted hummed, taking the words in. No judgement. Just encouragement. And kept on walking, at her pace. And without her bags weighing her down, the words bubbled up inside her and had nowhere to go but out.

"I adored her though. With the wild came such energy, such joy. Mentally… I don't know. My brothers remember the days in bed, the stints in care, which they shielded me from as much as they could. I'm mad at them for that, actually. For thinking I couldn't handle it."

"Mmm. Seems you are the lucky one for remembering her well."

"Ironic, that." A quick smile before she added, "I think that's why I love writing about people. Why I lean into their eccentricities. Why I want others to see those differences as marvellous, rather than something to shy away from. Because my mum was amazing. And difficult. And unrepentant. And she loved us so fiercely. If people can see past the hard stuff, to the hearts of other people, it can only make us more forgiving. More compassionate. I don't know. Does that sound like too much?"

"Adelaid, if you could hear yourself. It's not too much. You're not too much. You're marvellous yourself. Now, in what ways do you see *me* as marvellous?"

She looked to him then, really looked. "Are you okay?"

"Do I not seem okay?"

"You seem…high."

He grinned, and it was a miracle she didn't trip over her own tongue.

"I'm great. Fantastic even. Slept a treat last night. Am lighter for having seen my mother. Someone else is currently dealing with my emails.

And I'm strolling down this beautiful street on this lovely Melbourne day with you at my side."

He bumped her with a shoulder, and forgetting how big he was as compared with her, he knocked her sideways. Then reached out and caught her, hauling her back to his side.

And they walked that way, his arm around her shoulders, for several steps, before Adelaid had to extricate herself before she began to whimper with the pleasure.

"You might have all the time in the world for a stroll, but I have people to see, places to go. So, if you pass over my bags, we can find somewhere to sit and get cracking on our next interview."

But he wasn't having any of it. His gaze was sharp, his voice determined. "Not today. Today is me, Ted, getting to know you, Adelaid. I'm thinking we can start with the day you were born. What you were like when you were six. Any broken bones. Your first crush. Your favourite teacher. But as to the sitting and the eating, yes."

Handing her the cactus, he then took her by the other hand and dragged her down the street and into a restaurant.

Shocked into silence by the sparks travelling from his hands to hers, and settling around her heart, Adelaid could do nothing but follow.

Adelaid's legs jiggled madly as she watched Ted take off his glasses and toss them gently to the bar in which they'd found themselves. His cactus—as yet unnamed—sitting, protected, in the cradle between his elbows.

The place was dark and moody, all shiny wood and golden chandeliers. And somehow, once again, they'd picked a spot where her leg kept knocking against his, no matter how she sat.

Ted's thumb and forefinger rubbed over his eyes, as he groaned, "Now you're just pulling my leg."

"Nope. My brothers are all named after male leads in Doris Day movies." Adelaid lifted a hand to count on her fingers. "There's Brad, *Pillow Talk*. He's a plumber. Jake, *With Six You Get Eggroll*, he's an electrician. Wild Bill, *Calamity Jane*, he's a first responder. And Sid, *The Pajama Game*, is a cage fighter."

Ted looked up at that.

And it was the first time Adelaid had seen him without his glasses.

Unimpeded, the man's eyes were stunning. Beyond beautiful. He was beyond beautiful. The dim yellowy light rolled over his cheekbones like liquid gold, playing off the ends of his tangled lashes. The dips beneath his eyes were smudged—late nights, heavy burdens—and boasted a few creases at the corners. Making him seem less Clark Kent and more like a real live, flesh and blood man.

"A cage fighter," Ted intoned.

"He's a builder. I was just checking if you were still with me."

"I'm with you," he said, those eyes now hooked onto hers. His voice deep, and a little rough. "I've been with you since the very beginning."

Feeling light-headed, Adelaid asked, "What was the name of my fifth-grade teacher?"

"Mrs Hennessy. You were kidding about Wild Bill too, right?"

"Actual name on his actual birth certificate. Adelaid, one 'e,' is also from *Calamity Jane*. Have you seen it?"

He shook his head.

"Oh, you must! It's so wonderful. One of the best. Adelaid Adams is a glamorous showgirl. Secondary character though, which the boys never let me forget."

Deliberate too, Adelaid had long since thought. Her mum's funny way of conditioning her to never stop fighting to be seen, and heard.

Ted shook his head. Still without his glasses. Looking right at her. Nostrils flaring slightly, as he breathed out, hard. As if he just realised this was the first time they were seeing one another without anything getting in the way.

Needing to cut the tension, before it ate her alive, Adelaid waved a hand in front of his eyes. "Can you even see me without those things?"

He squinted. "You're a little blurry around the edges."

Ted leaned in, resting his forearm on the bar, his hand precariously close to her chest. "There," he said. "Now you're in focus again. I've never in my life seen anyone with eyes quite like yours, Adelaid Adams. I look into them and it's like I can see your whole life looking back at me."

Feeling restless, and overheated, and out of her depth, Adelaid started to lean back.

"Stop," he said, his voice gentle. But firm.

She stopped. But said, "I'm not a fan of being told what to do. Four older brothers, remember."

Ted lifted his hand and rubbed it over the corner of his mouth. "Were you aware that you have a habit of dropping truth bombs, trying to scare me off, any time you feel I might be getting too close?"

Adelaid swallowed. Then asked, "Whatever do you mean?"

"First your ADHD. Then the veiled threat of four older brothers. Just so you know, I'll call you on it, every time."

Adelaid blinked. So used to having to assert her right to take up space in the world was she, when her back was against the wall, she'd learned to push people away, before they could do the same to her. And it had been heartbreakingly easy.

Ted was the first person to ever look her in the eye and say, *I see what you are doing. I see why. And I'm not going anywhere.*

"Is this because of the politeness thing?" she rallied. "Is this you proving you can be sullen?"

He refused to bite. He waited till her eyes were once more locked onto his before saying, "This is me telling you that you're wonderful. And I like you. And I wanted you to know it."

"Ted."

"Why do you get to tell me, constantly, that I am polite, and clever, and cute, if I can't say that I think that you are lovely, and interesting, and driven, and bright, and lovely?"

She opened her mouth to tell him he'd called *her* lovely, twice, before she realised he was well aware. "When have I *ever* called you cute?"

Ted's mouth kicked up at one corner. Then he waved a hand over her, the way she had done to him more than once, making it all too clear she believed him empirically gorgeous.

"Whatever," she said.

"Not *whatever*," he said, his voice now deep enough to scare small children. "You own every opinion you ever have. You like me, Adelaid. You might even be nursing a little crush. Own that."

Heart now beating in her neck, her toes, the backs of her eyes, she scoffed, "Pfft. You, Ted Fincher, are not cute. You're…" She waved her hand again, taking in the swishy hair, the granite jaw, the warm eyes, the muscles, the height, the heft.

But it was the smirk that did it. The smirk that turned up the flame that had been burning inside of her from the moment she'd laid eyes on him.

One second she was mooning into his eyes, the

next she was overcome by the urge to wipe that smirk off his face. As if a pair of hands landed on her back and pressed her off her stool, Adelaid tipped forward, until her lips landed on his.

Eyes wide open she saw that his were open too. Open and lit with surprise.

Only by the time any of that made its way into the red fog inside her brain, Ted's eyes slowly closed, his hand had moved to cup her jaw, holding her with both tenderness, and intent. Holding her in place, he tipped his head ever so slightly to one side and kissed her back.

Only barely. A rush of air, a brush of lips. Like butterfly kisses. Till she found herself leaning deeper into his space, following the kiss, chasing it.

While around her, time itself seemed to slacken. To stretch. The world beyond Ted's hold, Ted's kisses, a blur of grey noise and smudged shadow and light.

Till Ted's fingers slid along her jaw, around the back of her neck, diving into her hair as he opened his mouth to play hers.

Drowning. Drowning in his heat and taste and skill, a small voice in the back of her head piped up asking what the hell she thought she was doing.

And she pulled back on a gasp. Breathless, trembling, her fingers lifting to her mouth to find it damp, swollen and aching.

What the heck was she thinking? So reckless. So impulsive. So much worse than footsies.

While she braved up enough to make eye contact, she found Ted smiling at her.

"Well, that's one way to own a crush," he said.

"Oh, shut up."

He held up both hands, in surrender. But the light in his eyes told her he planned to do anything but. There was an edge to him now. It wasn't just the lack of glasses. It was as if he'd been bitten by something that was making him bite back.

"Who are you, and what have you done with Ted Fincher?" she asked, still feeling a little feverish. What had got into him? What had got into her? "Did you cure something overnight? Did I make you walk too far? Are you hungry?"

"So hungry," he admitted, blinking and looking around for the first time since they'd sat down. "They serve food here, right? Not just beer nuts? Breakfast for my mother means nursing an espresso without drinking it."

Oh no. She knew how he was when he was hungry. Was it possible that all that just now wasn't about him burning with desire for her? He simply needed food.

Cheeks burning all the more with the realisation, Adelaid fussed about, sourcing a menu, put in an order, then watched him scoff down two large pub meals, while she sipped on a glass of iced water and stole his chips when he wasn't looking. Because she was a girl on a budget these days.

After a few minutes, his edge had been tamed, lost within a food fugue. "Is this the part where I get to say how grateful I am that you chose to do a profile on me? Not the other two monkeys, but me."

"No."

"When?"

"Never," she said, pushing his elbow so he'd keep eating. She needed that last little bit of glint in his eyes to disappear. In case it called to some other feverish part of her that had her straddling him at the bar.

"Why is that?" he said, a smile tugging at the corner of his mouth even as his gaze roved over her face, shamelessly, now that she'd kissed him.

"Because it's not…proper."

"Proper she says. And when did we land in a Jane Austen novel?"

When you kissed me the way Darcy might have kissed Elizabeth. With just enough reserve so as not to scare her off, yet such a rich slow burn that left her unsure as to how she'd ever truly lived before that moment.

"What we are doing here, together, with this profile," Adelaid somehow managed, "transcends gratitude. So stop flirting with me and eat."

And with one last smile that made Adelaid's toes curl, he finally did as he was told.

CHAPTER FIVE

THREE DOGS TUGGING hard enough on their leads to trip up someone less prepared, Adelaid wiped sweat from her eyes as they hauled her up the footpath. Didn't help that her mind wasn't exactly on the job. Hadn't been for the past few days, not when every waking moment had her reliving that kiss.

Not only her part in it—so reckless—but *Ted's*. Yes, she'd kissed him, but he'd sure as heck kissed her back. And it had been good. Dreamy-good. Keep a girl up at night, tangled in her bedsheets good.

Only while she'd felt as if she was burning up, he'd come out of it cool as a cucumber. As if her kiss had merely proven his crush theory, and nothing more.

Which, she supposed, was a good thing. For it wasn't as if the kiss could *go* anywhere. It wasn't as if the two of them could *be* anything.

There was their working relationship for one thing. While she was beholden to no one, and this was no "investigative" piece, and the entire point of her writing was to be affected and affecting, kissing her subject was still, probably, frowned upon.

Beyond that, Ted was wildly different from her. He was organised, on time, neat as a pin, while her work tote contained broken pencils, used lolly wrappers and sticky notes from three jobs ago.

She was also at a very different point in her life: hustling like crazy to get the slightest foothold on her dreams. While he was so successful, so well off, so far ahead in his field, dreamers only dreamed to be him.

Sensing Adelaid's lack of attention, the lead dog—a Shih tzu named Voltaire—darted left, towards the road and the park across from it. Instinct had her loosening the leads rather than tugging. The trio, losing tension on their leads, all but tripped over one another before straightening back onto the path.

Leaving her mind to trip straight back to Ted. And the small, hard ache inside, the knowledge that there was no point in starting anything as one day it would have to end. Not, for once, because the guy found her impossible to be with. But because they wanted very different futures.

She wanted a family, he did not.

Not that she saw every guy she met and thought—will he have babies with me one day? But Ted was different. He was spectacular. A good, strong, thoughtful, beautiful, weird and wonderful human being who looked at her as if she was pure delight.

That was possibly the worst of it. She'd finally found a man she liked, who clearly liked her back, who saw her ADHD as one small, *interesting* part of her rather than a huge red flag. And if things progressed past kissing, she was in danger of feeling way more than a crush. And fast. How could she not?

Making a mental note to write all of that down when she'd finished walking her neighbour's dogs, a bullet list, a big one, she looked both ways, then jogged the dogs across the road to the dog park, where she let them off leash to run to their hearts' content.

While she found a patch of shade and leant against the fence, working out how she might next get in touch with Ted. To line up their next interview.

For the time had come to wind it down. To get the story done.

Because, so far, no one was biting. She'd expected resistance. Her by-lines were suburban, rejection was par for the course. She wouldn't start worrying till she'd finished the piece and was on to her final pitch.

Her watch buzzed on her wrist, announcing a phone call.

Maybe, just maybe, this was the editor of her dreams offering to buy her story, right now! She pressed her earbuds to answer the call, her voice hopeful as she said, "Adelaid Adams!"

"Adelaid." Ted's deep voice rumbled over the phone, and Adelaid's knees gave out.

"I was just thinking about you."

"Were you now?"

Dammit. "About calling you to set up our next interview. In fact, having looked over my notes…" *and considering what happened last time we met* "…it might just be our last."

Ted's pause was telling. Or maybe she was projecting like crazy. Imagining his fist pressing into his chest, right over his heart, aching at the thought that soon they would have no reason to meet.

"When are you free?" she asked.

"Actually, I was calling to let you know I'm heading to the Gold Coast for a couple of days."

"Oh," she said, the single world dripping with disappointment.

"I've asked Hadley to keep an eye on Fuzz Lightyear, if that's your concern."

It wasn't. "Fuzz—?"

"My pet cactus."

Adelaid's heart lifted and fell with such suddenness it actually hurt when it landed. "You do know you only need to drip a little water on it, like once a week. Less is better. It takes very little work to make it happy. As for us, I mean, our next interview, do you want to get in touch when you're back?"

"That's the thing. There's room on the jet if you'd care to join me."

Adelaid blinked. "I'm sorry, did you say room on the *jet*? As in *private* jet?"

"I did." Into her silence he said, "I have a meeting with the lab I told you about, the one we are looking to acquire. I thought you might like to come along, see me in action. Two birds one stone." A pause, a clearing of the throat, then, "It'll be an overnight stay. Separate rooms, of course. If that's overstepping—"

"No. Not at all! I've never been on a private jet before. Or to the Gold Coast for that matter. We weren't exactly a 'going on a holiday' family growing up. Or 'plane people' for that matter." She stopped to take a breath. "You still there?"

"I'm not going anywhere."

As lines went, that one was like an arrow to the heart. Dead centre. Hitting the great push and pull of her life—craving her independence while dreaming of one day finding someone with stickability. Not that he meant it in that way. He was simply a good guy. Possibly even the best of the lot. Alas.

"Well, you are, actually," she said, keeping her voice bright. "To the Gold Coast. On a private jet. With me. I won't get in your way, I promise. I'll use our time wisely. In fact, I plan to use this opportunity to interview the heck out of you, Ted Fincher!"

"I look forward to it. Where are you now?" he asked in a voice that might have asked, *What are you wearing?*

"Dog park," she blurted, before it occurred to

her to say something more elegant and aspirational. "I walk them sometimes. Dogs, not parks. For extra money. It's something people do when they're not, you know, billionaires."

"Dog walker and writer," said Ted.

"And occasional bartender, barista, babysitter, tutor and writer for hire. There's good money being the subject of university experiments."

"Please tell me you're joking. About the last one. The rest sound like fun. Great ways to find fodder for your stories, I expect."

Adelaid looked to the sky for help. Her brothers saw her hustle as continued proof she needed minding. Ted saw it as integral to her career. It was really, truly, not fair.

He said, "I'll have a car pick you up in three hours."

"Great. And in case I forget to tell you later, thank you for inviting me along."

A chuckle. The kind that sent shivers through her limbs, the tingles settling right in her middle. "You're most welcome."

With that Ted rang off. Adelaid held her phone to her chest, let herself indulge in a few moments of ridiculous excitement. Then set to rounding up three small excitable dogs.

Bags over her shoulder, vintage trolley suitcase bouncing behind her on the tarmac, with the roar of the engine, the rush of wind and the aroma of jet fuel filling her senses, Adelaid might have been Katharine Hepburn striding to meet Howard Hughes.

Till she spotted Ted, grey suit doing its very best to contain his beastly size, one foot on the staircase leading up into the gorgeous Big Think jet, and everything else became white noise.

Yes, this was a working trip. And yes, she was fully prepared to pretend their kiss was an aberration. A mental hiccup on her part, hunger on his. But come on—a private jet, to the beach, with a gorgeous billionaire? She was allowed to lean into the frivolity, just a smidge.

When she reached Ted, his hand landed on her waist as he leaned in to kiss her cheek. Instinct took over, her eyes fluttering closed as his lips brushed the edge of her mouth.

A beat slunk by before either of them pulled back. Then their eyes met.

"Hey," he said, his voice a deep growl.

"Hi."

Then, before she could stop him, Ted relieved her of the handle of her suitcase—no request, it was just happening.

Only this time, she reached out, and grabbed it back. "Thanks," she said, "but I can look after myself."

His hand resting beside hers on the handle, he searched her eyes. And whatever he saw there had him nodding. "Of course."

Of course. Of course his little finger brushed hers as he let the bag go, and of course she felt that small touch all over her body.

"After you," he said, meaning she could feel him behind her as she dragged the heavy bag—*clunk-clunk-clunk*—up the stairs.

At the top, Adelaid peeked around the corner into the cabin and her mouth dropped open. Literally. For it was pure Tony Stark. All cream leather and dark wood trim, with lounge-looking chairs, TVs and fancy-looking gadgetry imbedded into the walls and, at the far end, a very well-stocked bar.

Ted eased around her, strode up the aisle and called out to the captain, Donna, and flight attendant, Stacey, so as to make introductions.

"Stacey, remind me to send you the link for Ms Adams's story about the twelve-year-old who collected enough aluminium cans to fund a soup kitchen for a year."

"You read that?" Adelaid asked.

"Of course. Research is what I do. Had to know what I was up against."

"I—" *Don't know what to say.*

"Champagne?" asked Stacey, holding the backs of the seats as she walked down the aisle.

Adelaid shook her head. "Water would be great."

Stacey smiled a knowing smile. "Get settled and I'll bring you both some lemon water, and a nice light meal, and with Mr Fincher as company you'll be golden."

Ted filled the aisle as he strolled back to meet her, his big hands holding the backs of the chairs nearest. "Don't hold back on my account. The booze on board is top notch."

"I'm working," Adelaid blurted. "This is a work trip. So best not."

"Rightio. Now, may I pop your suitcase in the overhead?"

Adelaid thought about it. About the way he'd paid attention to her desire to manage her own affairs. And how, considering his height and strength relative to hers, she'd be a fool to reject his offer.

"You may," she said, letting go of the handle well before he reached for it.

Once he'd double-checked the luggage hatch was secure he turned back to her. Then he huffed out a breath as he took her in. "In case I forget to tell you later," he said, his voice low and sexy, "I'm glad you came."

Adelaid did her all to control her faculties, but it really was all a bit much. The jet, the tension, the man. She could feel her chest rising and falling. Feel the heat creeping into her cheeks. Feel her fingers aching to fiddle with something. Anything. So that she didn't spontaneously combust.

"This is crazy posh, Ted!" she blurted, giving herself the chance to break eye contact.

"It is a bit much," said Ted, his hand running up the back of his neck. "And I'm not in love with the footprint. But I assuage my guilt in knowing the convenience means the work is served."

A timely reminder that his commitment was to his work. And only his work.

"I'd imagine," she said. "Not sure why I didn't think of it sooner."

"Mmm. Now go pick a seat," he said, moving to give her space. "Anywhere you like."

Adelaid tugged back the tension roiling through her and nodded. "Okay."

She went to move past Ted, only the man was so big there was no passing without feeling the heat of him all over, getting a lungful of his clean masculine scent. A slight panic overcoming her, she tried to turn back, but her shoulder bags twisted, leaving her stuck. Stuck up against Ted.

A glutton for punishment, she lifted her eyes to his to find they were about as close as two humans could be without it being entirely deliberate.

Her imagination went a little whackadoo at that point. Wondering what he might do if she grabbed a hunk of his shirt and dragged his mouth to hers. Or if she scraped her teeth along his stubbled jaw. Or sucked that bottom lip into her mouth and gave it a tug.

Then his gaze, all heat and intent, dropped to her mouth. And damn it if the man didn't lick his lips.

"Here's your lemon— Oh! Excuse me."

Adelaid turned to find Stacey hotfooting it back

up the aisle and behind the privacy screen. It was enough for her to yank her bags free and follow.

Dumping her shoulder bags on a random seat, she dumped her wobbly body beside them. Belted herself in. And wished she could bend at the waist and hold her head in the brace position for the entire flight.

"Look!"

Ted blinked and glanced up, the world beyond the edge of his computer, the neatly stacked reports he'd been rereading about the lab he was due to tour, coming into focus.

Adelaid—who'd moved about four times in the thirty minutes since they'd taken off—now sat in the seat facing his, a table between them.

"Look!" she said again, hands braced either side of the window.

He was looking. At Adelaid. Which had become one of his very favourite things to do. There was always so much going on. The flicks of hair that found a way to escape. The flush of adventure riding high on her cheeks. The heady attraction swimming in her liquid green eyes which made him feel like there was a fist permanently gripped around his lower spine.

She flicked him a glance, a crease popping in and out of existence above her nose. "Not at me. Out there."

"Right." Ted looked. *Out there.* They were

cruising above a carpet of cumulus cloud, the kind that usually meant relatively smooth flying. "What am I looking at exactly?"

"The insane blue of that sky. The perfect puffs of cloud. All of it," she said, her voice awash with awe. "I'm not religious, but damn. That's some miraculous stuff right there."

Ted looked harder, opening up a sliver of space in his brain to see the view as she did. Not the topography. Or the science of convection, pressure systems and refraction of light.

Looking at the view from her angle, through her eyes, it was indeed quite beautiful. It was meaningful due to nothing more than how it made a person feel.

It was something worth pausing for.

When he heard a sigh come from Adelaid's direction, his gaze moved back to her just as she faced him. Her eyes lit by that deep underground river of kinetic energy, right there for anyone who cared to look.

"Sorry," she said, wincing, "you were working. And I promised I wouldn't get in your way."

"It's fine. But you can interview the heck out of me *after* the lab visit. It's even in the schedule."

"Really?" she said on a laugh.

Ted pulled up the schedule on his phone and showed her. When she leaned in, he was suddenly back in that moment in the aisle when she'd tangled herself up in her bags. Her gaze warm and unfocussed. Her teeth worrying her bottom lip. She'd smelled like sunshine and sugar. Made his synapses misfire and his nerves tangle. To the point that he'd had to pinch himself in the side so as not to lean down and claim that bottom lip. Soothe it. Own it.

She smiled at seeing her name in his calendar, newly colour-coded and all, before her eyes lifted and tangled with his. Then she crossed her legs beneath the table, bumping them against his.

"Jeez, Ted," she said, pulling her leg away and wriggling to sit higher in her seat. "How do you cope?"

"With?"

"All those legs!" She reached out with a foot deliberately that time. The rounded toe of her shoe tapping at his shin. *Tap-tap-tap. Spark-spark-spark.* Like flint on steel.

"Last time I checked I had the regulation two."

"True. They're just so long, and big. Don't they get in the way?"

"Rarely." He shifted his legs under the table till he found hers.

"That was deliberate."

He smiled his answer. And for his efforts earned a slight bob of her throat, her pupils swarming into the soft green till there was nothing left.

"Pot calling the kettle black," he said.

"Are you accusing me of playing footsies with you? I'm…a wriggler. ADHD, remember? All that nervous energy has to go somewhere."

Ted kept his foot next to hers, watching her decide if she ought to move it, or leave it there. In the end she left it where it was.

Good decision.

Then she reached into one of her many bags and pulled out a container, before pushing it across the table towards him. "So your blood sugar is all good for your important meeting."

"Please tell me that's a muffin."

"Raspberry and white chocolate."

He opened the lid, pulled it out and took a bite. It tasted like heaven. "For a guy who's never had much of a sweet tooth I'm getting used to this."

She grinned. "You're evolving. Good for you."

He laughed, then went back to his reports. And if their legs happened to brush past one another several more times during the flight, neither of them said a thing.

Adelaid should have known the bubble would pop. It was the story of life with ADHD. Ups and downs, yin and yang, intense periods of productivity followed by complete psychic depletion.

After freshening up at their hotel, her room even more posh than the jet, they headed straight to the lab.

Shucking a lab coat over her vintage wool pants and high-collared button-down shirt made her look like an Oompa Loompa. Then she was off, sporting goggles, gloves, booties, and clutching a non-disclosure agreement she'd signed while on a video call with Hadley who had talked her through it; Adelaid tagged along behind the dozen others on the tour.

The lab was out of this world. All shiny surfaces and insane technology, and more big pointy things with "scope" at the end of the name than she could hope to remember, not that she was allowed to write about them.

And then there was Ted. The shiniest thing of all.

Yes, she'd spent time with Ted in his Dr Strange lair. She'd watched him work with his fancy computers and his neat rows of pencils, while wearing his serious face. She'd heard him on the phone, using his boss man phone voice, and it was hot as hell.

But here, in the wild, prowling through his natural environment, surrounded by groupies drooling over his every word, the man was king.

People came out of their offices to meet him, swarmed him like he'd just kicked the thousandth goal of his career and they were there to witness it. He asked cutting questions, drilled down hard into the answers he was given, with no compunction at all. He led the lab owners around their own space as if he owned it already. And they loved him for it.

Somehow, over the past weeks, she'd forgotten that *that* was the reason why she'd wanted to interview him in the first place. Not merely because he was a cute billionaire, and that kind of things sells,

or so that she might get to know the man behind
the name, but because he was a man of import.

His work was groundbreaking. His time infinitely precious.

He was Ted Freaking Fincher, literally saving
the world one discovery at a time.

Her small suburban dreams were nothing compared to his. Yes, they were valid. And important. To her. She'd fought for them, worked for
them, earned them.

But just because he kept a cactus alive, or enjoyed her muffins, didn't mean he was changing. Or able to change. His path was well-carved,
from hardest stone. Believing he might change
his mind, so that he could squish himself into the
small box she'd carved out for herself, was only
going to end in heartbreak.

Feeling like an overfull balloon that had suffered a tiny prick and was slowly deflating, Adelaid
slipped quietly away from the group and made her
way back outside into the bright beachy sunshine.

Finding a bench by a fountain in a small private
garden in which to wait out the tour, she slipped
off her mask, and gloves, and checked her phone.

There was a R-rated message from Georgette
in response to the news she wouldn't be home
that night.

And another from her oldest brother, Brad.

Called you at work. They said you don't work
there anymore. What the ever-loving hell, kid?

CHAPTER SIX

LATER THAT NIGHT, Adelaid stood on the balcony of her suite—not room, *suite*—looking out over the unimpeded ocean view: a half-moon casting silvery light over the cresting waves, and an eerie blue tinge on the curving horizon. And she felt more emotionally spent than she had let herself be in quite some time.

Her phone call with her brother had gone down pretty much as she'd have expected. Lots of sighing. A lack of understanding that she was working towards something more than simply being gainfully employed. Insistence she come to Sunday lunch.

Trying to convince Ted, when he'd found her in the garden, that she was just a little over-stimulated, that the lab was fabulous and that he was a rock star, hadn't gone down much better.

He'd looked at her with concern. Which she hated. She much preferred when he looked at her like she was magic.

She'd put on quite a show in order to get him to take her to dinner. So that she could finish off their final interview. He'd picked a burger and beer joint with warm, gentle lighting and a constant low hum of white noise, as if he'd known that was all she could handle. And it had taken everything she had not to fall in love with him then and there.

And there, sauce dripping from their fingers, she'd interviewed the heck out of the guy, as promised. No flirting, no distractions, no hunger issues, no segues, no footsies, no hand touching accidental or otherwise, no mistimed move that ended up with her in his arms.

And yet, now, standing on the balcony of her amazing suite in the most glamorous hotel, a gentle wisp of salty evening breeze playing over her warm skin, she felt hollow. Even a little morose. As if that overblown balloon had finally lost all of its air and was now just a blob of limp rubber.

Because after this her time with Ted was done.

"Hey."

As if she'd conjured him out of thin air, Adelaid looked sideways to find Ted standing several metres away. "You're on my balcony."

"It's a shared balcony, actually," he said, pointing a thumb towards the room behind him. "The company has permanent access to both suites, and they can be opened or closed as we see fit. I hope that's okay." He made to move, to move away.

"Stay," she said, her voice slightly breathless.

And he stayed. His pose was relaxed. The gentle breeze playing with his auburn hair.

He really was the most beautiful man she'd ever met. Way out of her league. Wanted none of the things she wanted most in her life. So utterly wrong for her.

All this she knew with every fibre of her being, and yet, in shortie pyjamas with a cactus motif, instead of her usual sartorial armour, she was completely unprotected. As such, she cocked her head, beckoning him to her side.

Ted's movements were unhurried as he walked across the wide expanse, past a big outdoor lounge and a huge private spa. He'd changed into old jeans that hung low and soft off his hips, an olive-coloured tee, and his feet were bare. His glasses were clear in the low light.

While Adelaid's heart began to beat like it had never beat before.

"Done for the night?" she asked.

He rubbed a hand over his face. "For now. Unfortunately, night and day are mere constructs when you run an international concern."

"Can I quote you on that?"

He looked to her, his face scrunching in chagrin. "Please don't. If not the most pretentious sentence to ever come out of my mouth I don't know what is."

"It's all good. You're just lucky you were a pro tonight. I have more than enough to finish out my piece," she said, taking her chance to drink in his profile. She'd looked up *aquiline*, only to find his nose didn't fit the description at all. Too straight, too fine, but her ancestors would have approved all the same.

His brow twitched, before he turned to face her. "So are we really done?"

"Mmm-hmm. Any last fact checks I can follow up with Hadley. I've taken up more than enough of your time."

He didn't say a thing. Just watched her. With the late-night stubble shading his granite jaw, his eyes dark in the half-light, it was a sensory barrage. *He* was a sensory barrage. But not the kind that sent her looking for a quiet dark place in which to recharge. The kind that made her feel like her blood was lit with static, the kind that left her wanting more.

Which accounted for her next words.

"This is the part where I say how grateful I am that I, Adelaid, got to know you, Ted." Her hand, which had at some point moved to cover her heart, lifted from her chest and moved to touch his. She stopped herself just in time, her fingers curling into her palm.

Till Ted reached out and caught her hand, his long blunt fingers wrapping around hers, before placing them gently over his heart. Her fingers splayed out, as if desperate to cover as much of him as they could.

"Can you feel that?" he asked, his voice rough. And so gentle she could hear the swish of the distant waves.

Though that could have been the sound of blood rushing by her ears as her heart worked overtime.

"If you mean your left pec," she said, "then sure. It's impressive."

"Adelaid."

"Where do you even find the time to work out? Because from what I am feeling right now, you work out."

"*Addy*," he said, in reproof. "I can see you are attempting the truth bomb thing again. Though you're either losing your touch, or you're just not trying as hard."

Her chest rose and fell, her lungs needing more air than they'd ever needed before, as panic swept over her. Panic and lust and feelings and more panic. "I don't know how you expect me to respond to that—"

"Muffin," he said.

"Muffin? As in you're hungry and want a muffin? Please don't tell me you're looking at me like that because you're hungry. Again!"

Ted's confusion was clear. "Muffin," he said, his voice a rough burr, "as in stop telling me what's what, and listen."

His fingers curled around hers, while still keeping them near his heart. And yes, she could feel it beating. Solid, strong, *whump-whump-whump*. His very life force. And soon it matched hers. Her pulse leaping at her temples, at her throat, in her belly and lower.

"My heart," he said, "hasn't been beating quite the same ever since you walked through my door."

Oh boy.

"I tried to explain it away at first, via the science. My decrease in appetite, raging insomnia, wandering mind—all of which point to higher than normal levels of dopamine and norepinephrine. Turns out they belong to the catecholamine family of hormones, which play a big part in the chemistry of attraction."

Adelaid was trying to keep up, she really was. But when his spare hand lifted to cup her cheek, his thumb caressing the curl of her ear, dislodging her loose scrunchie, which plopped to the floor, every sense bar touch was out of luck.

"They can make a person feel giddy," he said, moving in closer. "Energetic. Even euphoric. Any chance you've been feeling any of that of late?"

"I have ADHD," she blurted. "I feel those things all the time."

He sniffed out a laugh, then levelled her with a hot dark stare. Reminding her that he was not to be deterred. That he was way too smart for her usual tricks. That she didn't need to assert her right to take up space in his world, for he was more than willing to share.

Which made her feel brave enough, safe enough, to ask, "Are you, in your own inimitable Ted language, saying that you are attracted to me, and asking me if I might be attracted to you? Because I think the fact that I kissed you the other day pretty much gave me way."

The hand on her face delved deeper into her hair. His thumb playing gently over the edge of her mouth.

"Tell me what you are feeling," he said, close enough now his breath wafted over her ear.

Her mind tumbled. Her limbs trembled. Her eyes fluttered, but she forced them open. "I feel… everything."

He smiled, his killer smile, and she splintered into a thousand hot pulsing shards.

"May I kiss you, Adelaid Adams?"

"Are you always so bloody polite?" she managed, even as she curled her fingers into his shirt, dragging herself up his body.

"Not always," he growled, before he leaned down and traced his tongue over the seam of her lips.

Her bones lost all structure, yet her body tensed as if she'd been hit with an electric shock. When her mouth dropped open on a lush sigh, that was all he needed to claim her mouth with his.

While their first kiss had been sweet, gentle, tender, this kiss went from zero to wild in two point three seconds.

Adelaid gripped Ted's shirt hard as his tongue swept over hers. As his lips took her to heights she'd never known existed before, he also dragged her under with a litany of sweet, deep, drugging kisses.

She ran her hands over his big meaty shoulders, into his hair, down his arms, around his hips. Yanking his shirt free her hands swept up his back, digging into the smooth hot muscle, savouring his hardness, the shape of him, that'd had her feeling feverish for so long.

With a beastly groan, he cupped her backside and lifted her so that she might wrap her legs around him.

Which she did.

Her centre pressing up against the hard, long length of him, giving every indication the man's proportions continued under his clothes.

And when his arms embraced her, held her, protected her, Adelaid fell into Ted's kisses, heart first.

It was then that a tiny spark of sense flared to life. The reminder that she wasn't meant to be doing this. Wasn't meant to be kissing him, holding him, and she certainly wasn't meant to be feeling so many feelings for him.

"Wait," she managed, coming up for breath.

Rearing back, she nearly tipped out of his arms, but his hand ran up her back, scrunching up her T-shirt as he caught her, his palm finding bare skin. And she saw the moment he realised she was braless. His eyes dark as midnight, his jaw like rock, tendons strained in his neck.

But still he waited. Her word gold.

Then he hitched her a smidge higher and...

Holy moly.

Adelaid gripped Ted's biceps, pressed into what little give they would allow. Tried to stop her eyes from rolling back in her head from the feel of him. The heat of him through her thin pyjamas. Only to curl like a cat against his hand. Her body rocking into his out of pure instinct. And yearning. And need.

She wanted this. She wanted him.

What if this was not so much reckless as inevitable? And who said she had to be blameless all the damn time? Who said she wasn't allowed to make mistakes? Especially the kind she went into with eyes wide open.

She began to slip and Ted hitched her again, his hand dragging her shirt higher still, his eyes hot and apologetic.

So she rocked into him again, leaned forward to rain kisses along his jawline. "You taste so nice," she whispered.

"Nice?" he managed.

"Like the sugar I've been plying you with is dusted over your skin."

"Please tell me this means you've let me off the leash?" he said.

She leaned back just enough to whip her T-shirt

over her head, and tossed it over her shoulder, in the direction of the sea, wondering, for a half a second, if it might have gone over the balcony and right now be fluttering down the side of the building.

Then she slid her hand into his glossy auburn hair and demanded, "Kiss me, Ted."

And he did. He kissed her till she couldn't remember why waiting had ever been a consideration.

As he walked her into her suite, he murmured against her ear, "By the time I'm through with you, Adelaid Adams, the word *nice* will be so far down the list of words you decide to use to describe me, it may even fall off."

And he spent the night showing her how not nice he could be.

Adelaid sighed as her eyes tried to open. But the light was too bright. The mattress too soft. The arm pinning her to the bed Ted's.

Her eyes flung open. Her brain cataloguing the crash of surf, the murmur of traffic far below, balcony doors flung wide open, gauzy white curtains fluttering in the warm breeze. Warm even breaths tickling the back of her neck as Ted spooned her for all he was worth.

So, that had happened.

After circling one another for weeks, living with a slow burn that had felt sweeter and lovelier than any actual relationship she'd endured, *whoomph*! It had blown like a pressure cooker that had popped its lid. At least, she was the pressure cooker. His mouth on her, big blunt hands holding her wide, his tongue having its merry way, she'd blown for sure.

Biting her lip to stop from moaning at the memory, she lifted her head in the hopes of spying her clothes. Then dropped back to the bed when she remembered she'd flung her pyjama top goodness knew where. Leaving her topless when he'd tossed her to the bed. A gorgeous grin on his face as he'd whipped her pyjama bottoms from her legs in one go, the undies with them, proving his skill sets went way beyond human, and into wizard territory.

Everything from there was a blur. Kisses, caresses, the slide of hands, the sweep of tongues. All heat and sweat and bliss.

Thank goodness for Ted, who'd had provisions, for Adelaid wasn't on the pill. It exacerbated her symptoms. Badly. Ted had made sure they were safe, every time. And made sure *she* was aware that he was making sure of it.

The last thing *he* wanted was an accidental pregnancy.

Adelaid grimaced. *Nobody* wanted that. Including her. Even while she and her brothers were all the result of such folly, or so her mum had told her. And there was a memory Adelaid preferred had been lost to time.

Feeling abashed, and achy, and a little muddled in the cold hard light of day, Adelaid tried to extricate herself. A shower, some clothes and a few robust mantras tossed her way in the mirror would set her up better for facing him.

Facing whatever came next.

Moving, it turned out, was no small feat. For Ted was a cuddler. Every bit of skin he could manage to press up against her he did. And there was a lot of skin. Smooth, tanned, tight, toned skin. Some of it covered in a smattering of coarse dark hair. Then, as if she'd been thinking hard enough to rouse him, Ted moved. Stretching, his bicep brushing the edge of her breast, creating skitters in its wake, before his hand came searching till it found what it was looking for.

And while, admittedly, she could happily have stayed wrapped in his arms, his hand over her breast, his breath wafting over her ear playing havoc with her nerves, it had been a night out of time.

It was not real life. Neither could it be.

Focussed on the pair of freckles that lived either side of his old-fashioned watchband, she wrapped her fingers around his wrist, lifted the dead weight, then wriggled free.

Sitting on the edge of the huge hotel bed, the blankets on the floor, pillows askew, she looked back, half expecting to find those warm brown eyes looking back at her.

But on he slept. A hank of hair had fallen over half his face. His cheeks were flushed from the warmth of their bodies. The twist of the sheet revealed acres of hard muscular torso but draped just so over his groin.

He looked like a felled giant—all potential energy and brute strength. But his jaw was un-clenched, his mouth soft. As if the night before had given him a break from how hard he worked all the time. The man with self-confessed raging insomnia had slept. Because she was in his arms.

When her heart began to beat anew, and her belly tumbled over on itself in an effort to chase the feelings swelling inside of her, Ade-laid pressed herself up and off the bed, hurried over to her suitcase, picked an outfit from the clothes spilling out of the thing and hustled into the bathroom, breathing again only once she was on the other side of the door.

Maybe it had been reckless, thinking she could have him and walk away unharmed. Maybe it would still somehow bite her on the backside down the track. The thought of which reminded her Ted had done the same: flipping her over to nip her flesh, kneading away the pain, before lifting her hips and making it all better.

But she knew, right deep down inside, that she would never regret her night with Ted Fincher. Not for a moment. Not for the rest of her life.

Turned out, she needn't have worried about fac-ing Ted.

For by the time she was out of the bathroom,

Ted was gone, having left a note to say he'd had to take an emergency call about the lab, and could she be ready to leave by eight as their flight had been moved up, and had he mentioned two of the directors of the lab were joining them on the flight back?

Now in the car, on the way to her house, Ted continued to work. Having charmed the directors and sent them off in another car heading to Big Think, feeling well fed and deep in work mode, he was clearly in his happy place.

While Adelaid—itchy with sunburn from her quick beach walk after breakfast, and gritty from a lack of sleep, her nerves feeling more and more high-strung the longer they went without mention of the fact they'd been naked in one another's arms not all that many hours before—pretended to be intrigued by the suburbs dashing by past the car window.

She told herself that if he was cool about it, so was she. Or if not cool, then wishing she was. Which felt like nearly the same thing.

Adelaid's phone buzzed and she was happy to check her phone.

She found a slew of Call me! messages from Georgette.

Adelaid: In the car. On the way from airport.

Georgette: Was there one bed? Please tell me there was one bed.

Adelaid laughed, though it felt like a half-sob.

Adelaid: My room had one bed, not sure about his.

Georgette: :(

Adelaid glanced up to find they had turned into her street. She leaned forward, said to the driver, "It's just up there on the right. Jacaranda out front, pale green picket fence."

"Are we near?"

Adelaid spun to find Ted watching her, his big body at rest, reminding her how relaxed he'd been wrapped around her as she woke.

"Yep!" she squeaked. "Super close."

As the driver pulled a deft turn into her driveway Ted leaned to look out her window. His voice low, intimate, as he murmured, "Sorry we've not had a moment to ourselves this morning. I'd hoped we'd have more time."

"It's all good!" she said, whipping open the door, her foot already on the sidewalk before the car had rocked to a full stop. "It was a work trip. And you have a lot of people wanting a piece of you. You wouldn't have the position you have at Big Think if you weren't the guy."

When she glanced back it was to find he'd already hopped out of his side of the car. Where he pressed his fingers under his glasses, rubbing at his eyes, the first sign that he wasn't feeling quite as cool as she'd imagined. "I'm not the guy, Addy. Sawyer is the guy. Ronan is the guy."

Her fingers curled into a ball on the roof of the car. "Sorry to tell you, Ted, but while Sawyer can kick a ball and charm a room, and Ronan terrifies everyone into giving him what he wants, it's you out there saving the world."

"Addy," he said, his voice thick.

But she was already at the back of the car, waiting for the driver to pass her her case. Her toes scrunched, her fingers played with a belt loop, till she had her bags in hand.

And when the boot lid slammed shut, Ted was waiting for her. Hands loosely in the pockets of his suit pants, a gentle smile on his beautiful face.

When she tried to hitch her shoulder bags into a more comfortable position, while struggling with the handle of her suitcase, Ted held out a hand.

Letting go of a frustrated sigh, she stepped back, waited for Ted to slide the handle of her suitcase free, before walking it up onto the footpath. Sun glinted through the jacaranda leaves above, dappling his hair, his glasses. Creating a golden halo around his big body.

When he passed the handle to her, he moved in closer and used his now free hands to tidy the straps of her tote, her laptop bag and her handbag till they sat neatly on her shoulder.

"Thank you," she said.

"My pleasure" his gaze hot.

"Not for last night!" she said, her cheeks heating with the force of a thousand suns. "And not for this either." She motioned to the suitcase. The bags. "I could handle that on my own."

"I know you could," he said easily, a smile stretching across his face.

A breath in, a breath out, a sudden need to hold back tears. "I mean, thank you for allowing me the chance to get to know you, to have some insight into your work, your life. It's been a privilege."

His eyes narrowed before he offered a tight nod.

When he said nothing more, she looked away. Over her shoulder towards the house, expecting to see the curtains flicker.

Yes, he was mostly a man of few words, but she kind of wished he found some then. Which words, she couldn't say. She didn't dare try to fashion any inside of her head, lest they haunt her as soon as she walked away.

When she glanced back, readying to say goodbye, Ted took a step her way. That was all it took with those long legs of his. A single step.

Then his hand was behind her neck, and he was kissing her. A hard, hot, deep, sensuous kiss. In broad daylight. For all the world to see.

Adelaid felt her bags slump to the concrete as she let them go. Tipping up onto her toes she dragged her hands through his hair and kissed him as if she might never get the chance again.

An eon later, a millennia, Ted broke the kiss, pulling back to nuzzle her nose with his.

And Adelaid heard the buzz of his phone, growing louder and louder in his pocket. His world intruding. His work beckoning him back.

"You'd better go," she said, letting her fingers curl over his shirt before she forced some air between them. She could have sworn he placed a soft kiss atop her head before he moved away too.

"Adelaid," he said, his voice holding a note that felt far too bittersweet for her liking.

So she cut him off. "Now, Ted, this is the part where I go deep into my cave to get my story finished. Deep. It's the process, you understand? *I'll* call if I need any fact checks, otherwise I'll be deep. In the cave."

He nodded. Then with one last smile, the kind that made her heart catch, he stalked around the car, gave her a long look from the other side, slid into the back seat and was gone.

Leaving Adelaid standing on the footpath outside her house, a finger to her lips, feeling as if she had walked through some mirror into Wonderland where everything looked much the same, but was—quite simply—not.

And might never be again.

CHAPTER SEVEN

WHILE HADLEY AND Ronan snapped back and forth regards budgets, travel, staff benefits and the massive biyearly fundraising dinner Hadley was in charge of planning, Ted slumped in his dad's battered blue lounger in the Big Think founder meeting space, twisting his dad's watch around his wrist.

Life had snapped quickly back to normal after the Gold Coast trip. Normal meaning seventeen different projects suddenly requiring his rapt twenty-four-hour attention. Meaning reports to be read, funding approved, visits to labs in need of commendation or a shakedown.

He was swamped with fascinating, cutting-edge, eminently satisfying work, and yet the days had plodded slowly by. For "normal" also meant life without Adelaid Adams.

Adelaid had made it clear that she needed space to finish writing. That *she* would contact him if she needed him. Which she hadn't. Called, or needed him. And he *missed* her. Missed her smile, her mess, her electric energy. Missed her to distraction. More than distraction. To the point of physical discomfort.

He knew why. He'd done the research.

Oxytocin and vasopressin were now running rife throughout his system. The latter helped maintain blood volume and internal temperature, leaving him hot and cold, exhausted but wide awake, and as if his skin no longer fit quite right. It also played a role in regulating his circadian rhythm, his very sleep.

This, he'd read, was the attachment phase.

He sat forward and let his face fall into his hands. Rubbing life back into his face.

So what now? Following the science hadn't worked, so there was no point trying that again. Compartmentalisation hadn't worked. Exhausting himself hadn't worked.

The only thing that had given him any relief had been letting her in. Looking at the world through her eyes. Talking about whatever she wanted to talk about over burgers and beer. Holding her, having her, and having the best night's sleep he could ever remember. As if his psyche had been clenched for weeks and had been finally allowed to breathe out.

Only now it was somehow worse. Because he'd let her in and then blithely let her go.

But what was the alternative?

What if… What if he didn't let her in, but *in-*

vited her in? Made real space for her? What if he allowed himself the grace of actually *being* with her?

Adelaid had walked into his world and shaken it from the roots. There was no point looking at her with the same rules as he did for anyone else, for she lived by her own rules. She was independent, pragmatic and self-aware. She was also stubborn, and tough, and fierce. She was determined to assert her independence, and had passions of her own.

And she *knew him.* Knew his goals, knew his motivation. His ambition. And his limits. Knowing all that, she had opened her arms and let him in too.

A chair scraped and Ted flinched.

"So the profile," Ronan barked. "It's done?"

Ted lifted his head, looked at Ronan through bleary eyes. Tipped his glasses back onto his nose, and he sat up and said, "My part in it, yes."

"So it's back to business. Good."

Ted bristled, even though he was well used to Ronan's blunt focus. "I think you'll find I did manage to spend time with a woman and do business at the same time."

Ronan's pause was telling. "It's doable. I know. I plough through several—interviews, that is—a week. This one took you, what, a couple of months?"

"That's because Ted's not a 'wham bam thank

you ma'am' kind of guy," said Hadley. "And while you shoot sound bites at people, Ted was part of a profile requiring finesse, percolation. And wooing."

"Wooing." Ronan glanced at Hadley, then at Ted, as if suddenly noticing something was different about him. "Is that what's been happening here? Has there been wooing, between you and the writer?"

"Adelaid," Ted gritted out. "Her name is Adelaid. One 'e.'"

"Well, what do you know?" said Hadley, her eyes soft, her smile kind. Before she seemed to realise it and went back to lounging insouciantly in the doorway.

Ronan tapped a finger against his lips, his eyes hard. "Anything I need to know?"

Ted faced his friend. "Why? You looking for pointers?"

Hadley snorted, then rolled her eyes with enough elegance to make up for it. "Seriously. You," she said, pointing at Ted, "be nice. And you," she said, pointing at Ronan, "have no right to ask any of us what we do in our own private time. In fact, what the heck are we even doing here on a Saturday? Just because without Ted there is no Big Think does not mean he is married to his work. Day in, day out, like some automaton. Call me when you're done with the alpha crap. Till then I'll go back to running your company for you."

And then she left.

Leaving Ted and Ronan facing off.

"So," said Ronan, face unreadable bar the lift of a single eyebrow. "What now?"

Now Ted had to decide if he was going to be nice and polite and thoughtful and do what Adelaid had asked of him, and wait, or call her out for finding an excuse to push him away. Again.

Ronan said, "See if you can't get something in the piece about the wind energy start up in Tasmania. Help grease some government wheels for us!"

But Ted was already out the door.

Adelaid lifted out of her office chair to rotate Spikesarus Rex a half-turn on the windowsill, so that his thorny backside might get a little sun.

Then she plonked back down in the bouncy chair in the home office she shared with Georgette, and went back to staring through her laptop screen The Sinatra crooning through her earbuds was usually a winner at keeping her on task, but her muse just wasn't playing ball.

In fact, he hadn't been playing ball for the past couple of weeks while she'd been trying, desperately, to wrestle Ted's damn profile into shape.

Didn't help that her brothers were constantly beeping at her from the Adams family chat. Or that she'd taken on a bunch of extra busywork so as to fill the time she'd usually been spending researching Ted, or talking to Ted, or hanging out with Ted. Or that she'd been feeling off-colour. Bone tired. Foggy in the head.

The skeleton of the piece was there, the structure, the information. But what it was missing was the heart. The soul.

The Ted.

Because she was missing the Ted too.

She *knew* herself enough to know that giving in to her crush was not going to serve her.

It wasn't his fault. He'd been a total doll. He'd actually listened when she'd told him not to call, unlike others in her life who ran roughshod over any personal request she ever made. And he'd promised her nothing.

It was all her. Her and her tender, searching, hopeful, dreamy damn heart.

"Adelaid!"

Adelaid plucked the earbuds from her ears and looked over her shoulder. "Hmm?"

Georgette was balancing a pencil between top lip and nose, the Big Think Instagram page open on her mega monitor. "You're tapping your pencil against your mouth so hard you'll chip a tooth."

Adelaid stopped the tapping.

"What are you working on?" Georgette shuffled her wheelie chair over to Adelaid and squinted at the search page she had open.

Studies suggest oxytocin is the chemical messenger associated with trust, empathy, relationships. It's also used in sperm production...

"Adelaid?"

Oxytocin was also known as the love hormone. Not that she was about to tell Georgette.

Adelaid's head fell into her hands. "I'm stuck. Like, really stuck. I've tried all kinds of ways to find a way into the piece, but nothing is working!"

"Not even the R-rated stuff?"

Adelaid looked through her fingers and felt a blush rising up her neck. "I'm hardly going to tell the world he has a triptych of freckles along his hip bone."

Georgette grinned. "Pity. You'd make a packet!"

"This should be the easiest thing I've ever done. He's so easy to like and respect and his story is heartbreaking and heartwarming and he's so deeply real. I just need to get it all down in a vaguely readable way and it will sell. I know it."

"So, what's the problem?"

The problem? "I asked him to give me room so that I might finish writing. Without distraction. Two weeks ago. And he's actually done as I asked."

"The bastard."

Adelaid laughed, despite herself. "I know, right?"

"Can I help? We can brainstorm?"

The thing was, the person she'd become used to talking to about, well, everything was Ted. She'd become used to calling him up any time she thought of him. Sending him articles she thought he might find of interest. Knowing that, like her, he was up at odd hours. Like her, he was always happy to chat.

"I think I know what my problem is. I can't write about him because I miss him."

"Oh," said Georgette. Then. "Oh, my."

Indeed.

"So call him. Ask him out. Take the guy to a movie. How about that Hitchcock retrospective at the Avalon?"

Could she? Adelaid grabbed a printout of a particularly heart-stopping picture of him holding his glasses frames and looking just off camera, lab coat on, that hank of hair threatening to fall into his eyes. "He's Ted Freaking Fincher!"

Georgette shrugged. "And you're Adelaid Freaking Adams. I know you, darling heart. You're quick to retreat if you sense ambivalence. Meaning this guy must be as amazing as you've made out. And someone's gotta date him, so why can't it be you?"

Why couldn't it be her?

Because…because she liked him far too much. Enough that she was researching love hormones. Enough that she was having dreams about a future with a man whose vision of the future did not come close to matching her own.

The very thought had her stomach turning over on itself. Then it did so again. Imagining it must be anxiety, she closed her eyes and breathed through it till it settled.

Right then, a knock rattled the front door.

"I'll get it!" said Georgette, leaping from her chair. "Waiting on my book subscription. I'll leave you to your sperm 'research.' And romantic thoughts of Ted and—"

A creak of the front door was followed by Georgette saying, "You're not books."

A murmur in response. A deep, smooth, husky murmur that sent sparkly shivers down Adelaid's arms.

She rolled her chair to the doorway of office and poked out her head, to find Ted standing on her front porch in a white T-shirt, navy sports jacket, jeans riding low on his hips, the sheer size of him blocking out the watery sunlight.

It had been thirteen days since he'd dropped her home and driven away. Thirteen days since they'd spoken. Since they'd kissed. She'd had longer bouts between catch-ups with the man, yet this time, the yearning that filled her at the sight of him made her head swim.

Movement must have caught his eye as Ted looked over Georgette's head, his gaze clashing with hers. Heat and grit chasing one another through the warm brown depths.

"Addy," he said, his voice catching on her name. "May I come in?"

He fiddled with his dad's watch, as if riding a surfeit of energy. Currently picking at a tear in her old jeans, Adelaid felt a rush of endearment.

"Of course," she said, pressing out of the chair, "come on in."

Only then did her mind leap from the dishes piled in her sink, to the stretched-out Taylor Swift T-shirt a brother had given her for Christmas a zillion years ago, to the hair scrunched atop her head in a messy knotty bun.

Had she even brushed her teeth that morning? A quick swipe of tongue over teeth told her she had. Phew.

Georgette cleared her throat.

"Ted," said Adelaid, shaking her head in an effort clear a way through the fog, "this is my best friend, Georgette Gallagher. Georgette, this is Ted."

"Pleasure," said Ted, holding out a hand.

"Georgette works for Big Think's new PR firm and was the one who helped land me your interview."

"How so?"

"Funny story," said Georgette. "In her old job Addy had to write these top ten lists and was struggling to fulfil a brief entitled *Top Ten Sexy*

Single Billionaire Bachelors Under Forty. I mean, have you seen the state of the world's billionaires these days? It's rather dire. So she called me!"

Ted looked to Adelaid, who shrugged. There was no stopping Georgette at this point.

"'What about the Big Think guys?' I suggested, for the firm I work for had just been hired by you guys to do some freelance PR. 'Not sure if they're billionaires or merely millionaires, but according to the literature we've been commanded to learn off by heart they're right up there.'"

Georgette looked to Adelaid, encouraging her to take it from there.

"I looked you up," Adelaid said, her cheeks warming. "Found the source material highly curated. Controlled. And kind of dry. I thought you were crying out for my special touch."

Ted's cheek twitched. "Why me?"

"Two cocky alphas and a cinnamon roll. Which would you pick?"

At that he laughed.

"When she told me what she was thinking," said Georgette. "I dragged her into my boss, and she was given the green light within the day."

"And here we are," said Adelaid.

"Here we are," said Ted, his gaze stuck on Adelaid, his barrel chest rising and falling.

Georgette looked from one to the other before disappearing into the office, then coming out with her laptop. "So, I was just leaving. Nice to meet you, Ted. Keep up the good work. At work, I mean. Not when it comes to—"

She flapped a hand at Adelaid, then realised what she was intimating. Mouthing "sorry" a half-dozen times, Georgette finally slipped out the door, shutting it behind her.

Leaving Adelaid and Ted in a cloud of heavy silence.

"Would you like a tour?" Adelaid asked.

When he ran his hand up the back of his neck, she was nearly undone. "Sure."

"Not quite carbon negative," she said, motioning to the ancient light fixtures and the peeling wallpaper. "I bet you live in some fancy mansion, or penthouse, or Bat Tower." She glanced over her shoulder as they reached the sweet little kitchen that had made her fall in love with the place.

Though the pale yellow cabinets, gingham curtains and harlequin floor didn't seem to grab his interest quite so much as her face.

"I have a place in the city," he said. "Not far from Big Think. I'm rarely there. This," he said, eyes finally grazing over the second-hand kitchen stools and pictures of apples and oranges one of her nieces had painted now framed on her wall, "is much nicer. This is a home."

Something flashed over his face then. Some memory. Or some pain. And she remembered the way he'd spoken about his parents. About his cosy suburban upbringing. The kind she'd one day want for her own family.

Only the thought of kids, and Ted, brought with it a sharp jab of pain right through her middle. Shaking it off, she scooted past him, back into the hall.

Only, as she passed, his fingers curled warm and tight around hers and tugged her back.

"Why are you here, Ted?" she asked, needing to know. Needing to hear him say the words. "Was there something I forgot to ask? Some important hobby, or childhood memory?"

His thumb running over her wrist, his dark gaze roving over her face, he said, "Ronan would like a mention of our wind energy startup in Tasmania."

"Well," she said, her breaths now harder to come by, "we can't forget Tasmania."

With that Ted spun her against the wall, his big hot body trapping her there. "You asked me to wait," he said, his jaw tight, his voice subterranean. "So I waited. I waited long enough."

His hand hit the wall beside her head, as if he needed it to keep himself from touching her.

"If you want me to go," he said, his eyes on her mouth, "you're going to have to say the words."

His words were strong, but he looked ruffled. Unkempt. As if he hadn't shaved since—shock-horror—the day before. Considering all the crazy mental gymnastics that had been messing with her head, it was heady to think Ted might be feeling as out of his depth as she.

It was enough for her to admit, "I'm glad you came."

He breathed out, took off his glasses and put them on the small hall table that was perfectly within reach. Because he was a planner, her Ted.

Up close, his eyes were so clear. The whites a perfect white. She could fall into those eyes and never want to climb out. Maybe she already had.

She reached up, her thumb grazing the edge of his nose where his glasses had left a red mark. "What do you want from me, Ted? What are you hoping might happen between us? All evidence to the contrary, I'm not usually the kind of girl who sleeps with a guy, then doesn't call for two weeks."

His jaw twitched, his eyes roving over every inch of her face as if committing her to memory. "I was in the middle of a meeting, and then suddenly I was on my way here. That's not something that usually happens to me. *You're* not something that usually happens to me."

She made a noise. A soft sigh of yearning. Her hand reaching between them to give herself one last chance to stop this. To stop him. To protect herself. Only to cover his heart, while Ted sought out any last remnants of space between them and he filled it. Leaning in, infinitesimally. Overwhelmingly her completely.

Then his knee brushed the inside of hers, pressing them apart.

"How does it make you feel," he said, his voice like gravel. "Knowing I can't get through a day, an hour, without imagining what I'd like to do when I see you again."

"Tell me," she whispered. Turned out she was a masochist, after all. "Show me."

As if that was all he was waiting for, Ted leaned down to cover her mouth in a hot, open-mouthed kiss.

And the past two weeks of yearning, of missing, of reminding herself why going back to normal was the smart thing to do, turned to dust. Adelaid was lost. To touch. To feeling. To warmth. Sensation. Breath.

And after that first searing moment, as anticipation spun out into reality, the whole world gentled. Became more of a meeting, a testing, a tasting. Every slide of a hand considered. Every sip from one another's lips deliberate. Every moment so lovely, and sweet, it made her heart hurt.

So lost, was she, in Ted's hold, in his tenderness, when he pulled away, she whimpered, her mouth following his.

He made a rough noise in the back of his throat, before his hand swept over her cheek, his fingers delving into her hair, and he kissed her once more. The kind of kiss that could keep a girl going for days. Weeks. Months.

Then suddenly Ted was on the other side of the hall. His hair was a mess, his clothes askew. Most adorably, he squinted, just a little, as his glasses were out of reach. It took every bit of self-control not to rush him, jump him. Screw the consequences.

"I came here with a plan."

She rolled against her wall, and Ted pressed so hard against it the house groaned.

"I came to ask if you would like to go out with me. On a date. A proper date. Dinner? Drinks? A movie? All of the above? There is a Hitchcock retrospective not far from here—"

"Yes," she said, her voice lit with laughter.

"Yes?"

She nodded. Then laughed, the sound a burst of joy spilling from her. "Did you mean right now?"

"Absolutely." He swallowed. "If that's what you want."

The answer rang in her head. Crystal clear.

She wanted Ted.

She wanted to have him and hold him, and kiss him, and wake up in his arms. Only this time she wouldn't slip out from under his arm. This time she'd turn to him and kiss him awake and do it all over again.

She didn't want to be good, and sensible. She didn't want to think about the future. Not now. Not today.

Adelaid pushed away from the wall, held out

her hand, waited for Ted to place his palm in hers and led him to her bed.

Ted woke to find himself facedown, spread-eagled, in a too-small bed, his feet hanging over the end.

He opened an eye and came face to face with a pink fringed lamp, and a dog-eared biography of Judy Holliday. Squinting he made out shapes of floral wallpaper, a spring-green wicker chair covered in clothes, a small freestanding canary yellow wardrobe, doors wide open, boasting suits and dresses and hats and fancy shoes.

Adelaid.

Smiling, he rolled onto his back, stretched, then pulled the sheet with him, found his glasses on a chest of drawers and ventured out into the hall.

A quick search found Adelaid in her kitchen, music playing softly from another room. The morning sun pouring through the window glinted off wild wavy hair which spilled over her shoulders. A hand was wrapped around a huge mug, the other gripped her phone, a frown tugged at her nose, creating a pair of vertical lines between her brows.

His heart hurt just looking at her. But while at any other point in his life the very thought would have had him running for the hills, he breathed through it. Letting it simply be.

"Hey," he said, his voice rough.

She flinched, water leaping out of her mug and onto the floor. She mopped it with a small brown mat that was already on the floor, her gaze scooting from his face to his chest, to the sheet he had gripped low at his hip.

"Coffee?" she squeaked. "I didn't feel like it this morning, which is super weird. But I can make you some."

He went to her, leaned down, kissed her on the forehead. Then tipped her chin to kiss her on the mouth. "Good morning to you too. Sleep well?"

She levelled him with a look. For the neither of them had slept much at all. "Can you put some clothes on?"

"Why?" he asked. "Is Georgette about?"

"Well, no. She stayed at a friend's place last night. It's just obscene how cut you are, and I don't have the energy this early on a Sunday to suck in my stomach."

He slid his spare hand around her back. "I love your stomach. And your neck," he said, moving her hair aside so he could breathe her in, before scraping his teeth over that spot, just above her shoulder, that made her body roll. "And I'm quite partial to many of your other bits too. So, if you want to strip down, I'd have no complaints."

She leaned back, looked him in the eye and shook her head. He saw wonder in her gaze, disbelief, but also a spark, a sizzle. An undercurrent of heat and…something else. Something weighty and deep and rich. Something that rubbed up against big feelings inside of him in a way he'd never felt before.

"What's the plan for today?" he asked.

Twirling out from under his arm, she rinsed out her mug in the sink. "Nothing I can't get out of. Do you need help with anything? You said your place isn't as homely as mine. I can help you pick out a rug?"

"A rug."

"Unless you have some equation to complete, or disease to eradicate?"

He could see the erratic energy gathering in her eyes, hear it at the edges of her words. She was stressing about something. This time he knew it wasn't him.

"Want to tell me what's going on?"

Her mouth twisted. "Family lunch. One which I'm trying to get out of."

Ted's mind shuffled through the times she'd spoken of her family. Sunday lunches had been mentioned. Multiple nieces and nephews. Overbearing older brothers. Fond exasperation.

"Is family lunch a bad thing?" he asked, thinking that, as an only child who missed his father every day, it might have been something he'd rather have liked.

"No." A pause, then, "We eat a lot and laugh a lot. I get to cuddle my zillion nieces and nephews, and spend the rest of the time trying not to get cornered by my brothers, each of whom will take the chance to demand updates on my health, my living situation, my finances, my career, my life."

"What's wrong with your life?"

"Not a thing!" Adelaid's hands came together, fingers twisting.

"Can't you simply say no?"

"To...lunch?" Adelaid laughed. The laughter turning slightly hysterical. Then she clicked her fingers. "That's right. You're an only child."

Truth bomb, he thought, seeing the fight in her eyes.

Only this time he actually did put it down to her ADHD, ramping up due to stress. He'd read into it. Deeply. Since knowing her.

"True," he said, his voice low, gentle. "But I've known Ronan and Sawyer since I was seventeen. When punching each other in the arm every chance they got was their idea of kinship. So I have some idea of what it's like."

Adelaid's fretful hands slowed.

"While a new rug sounds great, consider option number two," said Ted. "Would you like company? A bodyguard? A distraction? Someone to hold your bags?"

"You want to come to family lunch?" she said, her liquid green eyes watching him, carefully. "With my brothers. And their wives. And their kids."

"There will be food there, right?"

"So much food."

"You know how I feel about food."

Adelaid breathed out, her gaze settling. "That's a nice offer, Ted. But I'm afraid my brothers would eat you alive."

"Brad, *Pillow Talk*. Jake, *With Six You Get Eggroll*. Wild Bill, *Calamity Jane*. And Sid, *The Pajama Game*."

Her mouth popped open. "How do you—"

He tapped the side of his head. "Good memory. For things I want to remember. I may even have watched two out of the four films."

Adelaid's hand went to her heart, her mouth popping open in surprise.

"I've had time on my hands the past couple of weeks," he said, moving in closer and pulling himself up to his full six feet five inches, barefoot. "Thank you for the warning about your brothers. But I can take 'em."

At that she barked out a laugh. "I'm sure you'd put up a good show. You're clearly very strong. And manly. It's just… I've never brought a guy to family lunch before."

She let that fall between them like a stone dropped into a pond, ripples bouncing off the edges of the room.

"They would make assumptions."

Ted took her by the hand and hauled her to him. "Let 'em."

Adelaid's eyes flickered between his, but she

gave nothing away. Breathed in. Swallowed. Nodded. Then a smile crossed her face. Like sunshine on a cloudy day. "Are you even free?"

"I'm free."

He wasn't. He was never free. Hadn't been *free* since he'd made a promise to himself, and his "brothers," when he was nineteen years old. Yet he was not ready to leave her.

Not yet.

Not ever, a voice rumbled in the back of his head.

He moved in, curled a wave of her wild blond hair around his finger. Using it to tug himself closer as he leaned down to kiss her. Stopping a smidge before his lips met hers. "What time is lunch?"

"Lunchtime."

"What time is it now?"

"Barely breakfast."

Ted opened his sheet and wrapped her in it.

And that was all it took for her to grab him and kiss him and climb him, and if they made it to lunch it would be a miracle.

CHAPTER EIGHT

ADELAID STOOD ON her brother Brad's porch, her usual bag of marinated chicken wings in hand. She told herself to knock, but her hand wouldn't move. It had been weeks since she'd shown her face at Sunday lunch. What with quitting, and all her part-time jobs, and Ted, it had felt easier, more politic, to stay away.

Ted moved in closer beside her, as if he could feel her rising tension and just wanted her to know he was there. His thumb running down the edge of hers. Calming her. Smoothing down her spiky edges. Only to leave room for a rush of feeling—longing, adoration, gratitude, wonder, disbelief, panic and something deep and sweeping—that made the backs of her knees threaten to give out.

These were not things she needed to be feeling now, right as she was about to enter the lion's den. Her brothers would smell blood, and it would be hell.

She squeezed Ted's hand, then let it go to knock on the door.

Jake, her second-oldest brother, opened the door, a baby on his hip, a toddler wrapped around his leg.

"Thank heck you're here. Take a kid." Jake unwrapped the toddler from around his leg and gave the kid's hand to Adelaid.

She crossed her eyes and curled her tongue at her nephew, till he became focussed on trying to do it back.

Then Jake saw Ted. He reared back and said, "You brought a dude? Bold move." Before promptly handing the baby to Ted.

"Wait—" said Adelaid, wiping a hand already sticky with toddler down the side of her jeans.

But Jake was already gone, calling out, "Hey, everyone! Addy brought a boy!"

Adelaid looked to Ted, to find him holding the baby at near arm's length. His face blank, his eyes wide. It would have been funny if not for the resultant ache in Adelaid's belly. A timely reminder that they wanted different things.

Not that her stomach was listening. In fact, the scent of the chicken had been making her feel funny the whole way over. The sooner she passed it off, the better.

"You okay over there, bud?" she asked.

Ted blinked, his deep brown gaze turning to her. "Yep. Fine." Then some dormant human instinct kicked in and he brought the baby to his hip. "And who is this?"

"Ted, meet Bianca, my brother Brad's youngest." Poor kid had inherited Brad's perma-frown. "There's a dozen more inside. We Adamses are prolific breeders. Still think you can take my family?"

Ted leaned in when the baby lifted a chubby hand towards his glasses, letting her smear and stroke and poke. "I'm currently adjusting my expectations."

Adelaid, on the other hand, was doing everything in her power *not* to adjust hers. But seeing Ted smile and goo, eyes twinkling at little Bianca, her insides fluttered and did cartwheels, before settling into a strange uncomfortable cramp.

He would be such a good father. So patient and focussed. So sweet and kind. So protective of those he loved. She pictured him researching prams and paediatricians. Setting up a creche at Big Think. They had entire spare floors in the building, after all. It really, truly, wasn't fair to humankind that he had cut himself off from the possibility.

Ted glanced over, his expression quizzical.

Adelaid looked away, hoping her yearning wasn't written all over her face. "Come on! No one can hit you when you have a babe in arms, so we couldn't have planned this better."

With that, Adelaid led Ted down the hall, waving to her huge extended family—Brad's wife, Betty, swooping in to relieve Ted of her child, Joey bolting off to find younger victims to poke his tongue at.

They made it to the kitchen in one piece. The room was filled with Adamses. Wives, girlfriends, cousins, kids. Working around one another as they covered the kitchen dining table in more food than any household could eat in a week.

"Everyone, this is Ted," she called. "Ted, this is everyone."

"Hey, Ted," said Sid's girlfriend, Sally, taking the proffered bag of chicken wings, before shooting Adelaid a look of *You go, girl*. Adelaid then motioned for Ted to follow her to the sink. Where they took turns washing sticky kid stuff off their hands.

He turned on the tap. She held out the liquid soap and squelched a bob into his palm. Side by side, they scrubbed their hands long enough they could have performed a surgery. Once done, Ted used the tea towel to dry his hands before passing it to her, smiling down at her, his face close enough she could make out the myriad colours in his hair.

And Adelaid realised how much she'd come to treasure the pockets of time when it was just the two of them, in a bubble, leaning into their attraction, playing "what if?".

And she let herself imagine what that might

look like as a reality. As a *future*. Living together, dining together, travelling together, snuggled up on the couch together, him reading his reports, her editing a piece she was writing. It felt peaceful, and warm, and lovely.

But then her twin nephews ran through the kitchen, screaming blue murder at one another, and the spike of joy, of belonging, of longing that pierced her was enough to make her moan.

"Scoot," Wild Bill's wife, Wendy, said, squeezing between them to wash the celery for the Waldorf salad.

Once she moved off, Adelaid turned off the tap with a little too much vigour and twirled the tea towel around both hands, using them as a shield to put a little room between herself and Ted. "Let me know if you're ready to bolt. We can sneak out the back door. So long as they have my chicken wings they won't care."

Ted moved in closer, and leaned his backside against the sink, tipping his head to hers to be heard above the white noise of the busy kitchen. "I get the distinct feeling you're preparing me for failure. Yet I'm not sure how a person fails at lunch. Unless it's by missing one's mouth with one's fork."

It was Adelaid's turn to narrow her eyes at him. "You've never walked into a room, not once, in your whole life, and been concerned at how people will receive you, have you?"

He opened his mouth. Closed it. This time when his eyes narrowed it was out of concern. "Have you?"

"Oh, my gosh. Constantly!" Her arms flew out, the end of the tea towel whipping through the air with a whip crack. "That's the story of my life, Ted. It takes work to hold in my fidgets, and constant effort not to feel overwhelmed. Even then people sense it. And judge. And make things harder. It's why this mob are so protective of me. Why family is so important to me."

Her eye caught on the kitchen doorway as the last of the wives, girlfriends, cousins and kids disappeared through it holding food and the related accoutrements, only to find all four of her brothers standing in the kitchen doorway staring at her.

"Took you long enough," she said, her voice tensing, as if preparing to battle. "Boys, this is my friend Ted Fincher." Only the slightest pause before the word *friend*, but she saw every one of her brothers clock it. "Ted, my sorry excuses for brothers."

Wild Bill, the quiet one, stepped up first, but only because Sid, the youngest, had given him a shove. "I'm Bill."

"Pleased to meet you," said Ted, leaning forward to shake Wild Bill's hand, while simultaneously slipping down against the bench a smidge so as to bring himself down to his height.

"Sid," said Sid, squeezing in to pump Ted's hand hard enough his knuckles turned white. "I'm the cage fighter, so you'd better be nice to my sister, or else."

"Ah," said Ted, "Adelaid already got me with that one."

Sid's mouth twitched. "She's told you about us, eh? What'd she say?"

"That there are four of you," said Ted, diplomatically.

Sid snorted. "Good one."

"We grew up with her, remember?" said Jake, taking his turn to shake hands. "Talks ten to the dozen ninety percent of the time. Doubt that's all there was to it." Jake's arms were crossed over his chest. And was he flexing? Jeez, he was totally flexing.

Adelaid rolled her eyes so hard they hurt. "Stop fluffing your feathers like nervy roosters. Ted is far too savvy to fall for your antics."

"Did you say your name was Fincher?" That was big brother Brad—the oldest, the frowniest and most likely to go full protector. "As in Big Think?"

Adelaid gawped. How the heck—?

"I'm a massive Sawyer Mahoney fan. Just missed out on a signed jersey at a charity auction once. Biggest regret of my life."

Ah. That made more sense.

"I'd be happy to send you something when

Sawyer's back in town. Might not have played for a while, but he still loves to give an autograph."

Brad nodded.

Ted nodded back.

"Now," said Brad, "tell us what the heck makes you think you're good enough for our sister."

Jake laughed. Sid grinned. Wild Bill shrank. While Brad cracked his knuckles. Literally cracked his knuckles. And while white noise permeated from the house beyond—kids playing, women laughing—the kitchen was dead silent.

Ted moved in so that his hand was resting on the kitchen bench behind Adelaid's back, his thumb tickling at her spine, as he said, "She invited me here today, and I trust her judgement. Otherwise, I'm not sure how you want me to answer that."

"Are you kidding me?" Adelaid muttered, shooting Ted a glance as she moved away from the bench. His touch not helping. Especially when she could feel him responding to the testosterone leeching through the room.

The last thing she wanted was for him to think he needed to start fighting her battles for her too.

Without thinking about it too much, she followed her gut. Ignoring her brothers and focussing on Ted. She clicked her fingers in front of his eyes. Watched as the fog cleared and his warm brown gaze focussed on her.

Then she shook her head.

He ran his spare hand over the bottom half of his face, his eyes flickering with chagrin. Before he gave her a half-blink. Of understanding. And acceptance. Just like that.

Before she could unpack how that made her feel, how his instant understanding layered over everything else she adored about him, Brad's wife, Betty, called out from the next room.

"Come and get it!"

Adelaid turned to see her brothers leaving the kitchen, noses lifted following the scent like Looney Tunes characters. Food taking precedence over deciding who was alpha gorilla, always.

"So that was my brothers," said Adelaid.

"I like them."

Adelaid laughed. Then realised he meant it.

Ted's eyes glinted as his hand swept around her waist pulling her closer now that they were alone. "They are clearly very fond of you, which endears them to me."

"Fond? Boy, oh, boy, are you an only child."

Rather than calling her out for pulling a truth bomb move, Ted slung an arm around Adelaid's neck and pulled her in for a quick kiss that soon turned into a long kiss.

"I can smell chicken," he murmured against her mouth. "Lead me to the chicken."

Knowing he'd only continue being of use to her so long as he was fed, Adelaid led Ted to the chicken.

Adelaid managed to sit through lunch, but didn't quite feel as if she was really there.

Ted was a dream. The wives and girlfriends all watched him goo-goo-eyed. Her brothers became more and more smitten with him the more Sawyer Mahoney stories he told. And after a while he stopped flinching every time a child screamed.

But every time someone passed a bowl of potato salad or a pasta dish under her nose her stomach turned. Till after a while she started holding her breath any time someone called out "Pass the gravy!"

"Adelaid?"

"Hmm?" she said, and turned to find Betty tapping her on the shoulder.

"Sorry, hon, I said can you take the baby? I really have to pee."

"Of course." Adelaid took baby, Bianca, turning her so she could face the table, and gave her a napkin to play with. Without thinking she sniffed her baby head, kissed her baby hair and made goo-goo noises into her baby ear.

And then, like a fog rolling in off a stormy sea, Adelaid's feet felt numb, her ears could only hear a strange whooshing sound and she held her breath to hold back the wave of nausea that had swarmed over her.

Passing Bianca onto whoever was sitting at her left, she excused herself and walked as normally as she could through the house.

Her mind now a constant flicker of images of her past few days. Her foggy head. The fact she'd been in bed before nine every night that week. How she'd not been able to stomach the idea of coffee that morning.

She was heading upstairs when she banged into Betty coming the other way.

"You okay, hon?"

"Yep. Bianca is with someone."

"You don't look so good."

"I'm fine." She wasn't. "Look, can I ask you something and you promise you will not tell my brothers?"

Betty's eyes widened in glee. "Please. It's been so long since I've heard any adult gossip I'm nearly dying of starvation."

"Do you happen to have a pregnancy test?"

Betty rolled her eyes. "Are you kidding? You know how often someone in this family pops out a kid. I have a set in every bathroom in the house." Betty looked over Adelaid's shoulder. "Who's it for? Janet? She's looking a little bloated."

Adelaid breathed out, nausea swelling inside her again.

Betty's eyes widened. "Oh. Oh, I see." She grabbed Adelaid by the arm and dragged her back up the stairs and into her en suite bathroom. A quick rifle through a drawer pulled up three different kinds.

"This one is most accurate soonest. That suit?"

Adelaid nodded.

"Don't look so worried, hon. It'll all be okay, no matter what. I know we've just met your Ted, but, Addy, he seems like a dream. And hot. But sweet, you know? As for you, the whole lot of us have been itching for the day we can return the favour and help look after your little ones. You know that, right?"

Adelaid nodded again.

"So, I'll leave you to it, shall I?"

"Thanks."

Four minutes later, sitting on the closed lid of the upstairs toilet, Adelaid stared at the fist gripping tight to the pregnancy test.

Her right leg jiggled. Her mind spun in circles. Had she really said, to Ted, *We Adamses are prolific breeders*? Her ovaries squeezing when she'd seen him smile at her niece. Was it possible she'd manifested her symptoms, so acute her desire for such an outcome?

No. This was not wishful thinking. She wanted a family. But not like this. Not while renting. Working a bunch of casual jobs. And sleeping with a man with whom she'd yet to go on an actual date.

She'd worked hard to make good choices in her life. To manage her condition. To surround herself with people who were kind to her. To create a safe space for herself.

So how had it come to this? Possibly, accidentally pregnant—the flakiest, most reckless, most Vivian thing she could possibly do.

Her breaths started to shallow, her skin prickling, as some of the harder memories of her childhood bled through, the ones she preferred not to focus on. Trying to wake her mum to take her to school, having to pack up and move while the landlord shouted about debt collection and leg breakers, her mum crying at the supermarket while trying to decide between bread or milk for her five babies.

Adelaid closed her eyes, breathed deep. It was not the same thing. She was not her mum.

And she'd done nothing wrong. Nothing bar developed feelings, strong feelings, deep, rich, romantic, soul-deep feelings, for the most excellent man she had ever had the privilege of knowing.

She was in a good place mentally. She was financially stable. At the moment. But if she didn't land on her feet with her shift in career, then that nest egg would start to deplete and fast. But she had a home. Friends. She had support, if she wanted it. For all that her brothers drove her crazy, she only had to say the word and her entire family would step up. For the first time in a long time that felt not like a burden but such luck.

And she had Ted.

Oh, Ted.

This was not what he wanted. Not now, and

not in some distant dream future. It was explicitly *not* his plan. Yet, she knew he'd be kind. He'd step up. Not like her mum's boyfriends, who'd all fled at the first sign of trouble. Not like her own father had.

The alarm on her phone went off. Keeping all of the above firmly in mind, her fist loosened. She slowly opened her fingers.

And felt a kind of preternatural calm as she focussed on those two bright pink *positive* lines.

"Holy mother of monkeys," she muttered.

"What? What does it say?"

Adelaid nearly jumped out of her skin as Betty's voice called through the door.

"Can you give me a minute?" Adelaid managed.

"It's positive," someone whispered. "Or else she'd have said so. Right?"

"Is someone else there?" Adelaid asked.

"Ah, it's me. Wendy."

"Betty! You promised you'd keep this a secret."

A shadow bled under the door, as if Betty was right there. "You said not to tell your *brothers*. And they're all downstairs, mooning over your baby daddy."

Adelaid's face fell into her spare hand, and she began to laugh. For it was laugh or cry, really, with her family. And damn sure she wasn't about to spend her first moments with her possible future baby blubbing with tears.

"Are you okay, hon?" Betty asked.

"Yep. I'm fine and dandy."

"We'll leave you to it, okay? Our lips are sealed from this moment on."

"Great. Ta." Adelaid heard the bedroom door swing open and closed and was alone.

Except, according to the two pink lines staring prettily back at her, she'd never be alone again. She was having a baby.

A person of her own. Who would love her, no matter her flaws, just as she'd loved her own mum. No matter what.

Well aware that mental health issues, and conditions such as ADHD, could be hereditary, Adelaid was not concerned on that score. Who better to raise a neurodiverse child than a mother who was informed? If the chips fell that way, she would be the most supportive, open-minded, adoring mother ever.

And then there as the fact that the child would be half Ted.

A teeny person who would inherit his kindness, his gentleness, his scintillating mind, his loyalty, his drive. But probably also the way he forgot to eat, and his anal relationship with time.

A mix of the weird and the wonderful, from both of them.

Ted.

She had to tell Ted. Had to pull the rug out from under him. Change his life for ever.

But not here. Not surrounded by her family. It wouldn't be fair.

None of this was fair. Not the least of which was the fact that they'd only just started getting to know one another. Or that she was about to drop a real metaphorical grenade on the guy that he could not clever his way out of.

Later. Away from here. She'd just have to get through the afternoon without giving herself away.

Hyper-focus could be a burden, but it could also be a gift. Especially when one really needed to finish an article one had been trying to write for weeks.

The evening before, after making it through lunch, Adelaid had felt like she'd been in a pillow fight—exhausted and slightly battered all over. Ted had offered to drive her home and let her get a proper night's sleep.

When he'd kissed her goodnight, turning her to mush on her front porch, it had taken everything she had not to tell him then and there. Or drag him inside.

But she resisted. Not without another test. Not till she was sure.

For it would change everything. Everything. For ever.

After sending him on his way, a kind of mania had come over her, a second wind keeping her up all night, writing till her shoulder ached, till her little finger of her mouse hand had gone numb, and till she could see the shape of the story as if it were a three-dimensional, living thing.

And then it was done.

No wave of relief or pride. Just exhaustion and a bittersweet sense of loss. That the reason they had come together was no more.

Yawning, spent, she'd sent it off at four in the morning—to Georgette, to Georgette's boss and to the Big Think lawyers for pre-approval. After they'd taken their bites, she'd show Ted. Then send samples out into the big wide world, her final chance to lure someone who loved it as much as she did.

Clocks had never held much sway over Adelaid, but now as she lay on the lounge awaiting a different kind of result—after dragging herself to the doctor for a blood test, and pamphlets, and a sample of prenatal vitamins—it was as if she could now hear one *ticking* permanently inside her head.

Leading to what? News? Or an end? Or a beginning?

Her phone pinged. Heart beating in her throat she turned it over.

Positive. Double-checked. Official.

She dragged herself to sitting. Her hand resting over her belly for a few private moments. Eyes closed she sent a message through her arm to the cells miraculously dividing inside of her.

You and me, kid. Anything else is gravy. But you and me? We'll be okay.

Opening her eyes, she dialled Ted's number to set up a time she could see him. So, she could tell him—

He answered all but instantly.

"Adelaid," he said, clearly glad to hear from her. "I just heard."

Her heart beat behind her ears. "Heard?"

"You're finished! Hadley got a ping from contracts. When do I get to read it?"

"Oh. The profile. Now, if you'd like. As soon as you want it."

He laughed, the sound so easy, so free. "I'm so proud of you, sweetheart."

Sweetheart. He'd called her his sweetheart. That was where they were in their relationship: the bright, beautiful, trouble-free beginning.

"I'm pregnant."

Adelaid smacked her hand over her mouth.

When she heard nothing but silence on the other end of the phone, she murmured, "Ted?"

"I'm here. Did you just say—"

"I'm pregnant. I'm so sorry. I had no intention of blurting it out like that. I wanted to tell you in person, but you were saying such nice things, and I couldn't sit here, feeling like I was keeping something from you—"

"Addy."

Adelaid breathed fast, and deep, diaphragm deep, attempting to clear some of the static in her head. "I made you a promise that I wouldn't get in your way. And I have. I'm pregnant, and that's going to change everything for you. When you were so clear that it's not what you want. I'm so, so sorry—"

"No," said Ted. His voice cutting through the loud grey glitter in her mind like a clash of symbols. "Hell, Addy. You have nothing to apologise for. I—"

She pictured him running a hand up the back of his head. Wished she could curl up on his lap while he did so. And kiss his jawline. And hold him tight. And for him to tell *her* everything was going to be okay.

"Where are you?" he asked, his voice calmer than he must have felt.

"Home."

"I'm coming to get you."

She shook her head, then remembered he couldn't see her. "Please. Do what you need to do today, then maybe come over later? After work. And we can talk then?"

"Okay. And, Addy—"

Adelaid pressed her phone as close to her ear as it would go. "Yes, Ted?"

"It'll be okay. I promise."

She nodded again before hanging up. The

words not giving the comfort she'd hoped, for that time the *sweetheart* was missing.

Ted sat on his dad's couch. Leaning forward, his head in his hands. He'd been there for a good half-hour, in the exact same position, working himself up to speak.

"Hey," he said, his voice croaky. For it had been years since he'd spoken to his dad. Longer since his dad had been around to speak back.

Ted ran his hands down his face and leant back in the chair. When he'd first dragged it with him to university, attaching it to the roof rack of his old Cortina, it had his father's impression in the back, his handprint on the arm. Now, it no longer bore signs of anyone's use bar his own.

"Dad," he tried again, "turns out there's a chance, all things going well, that in a few months from now you're going to be a granddad."

Or would it have been Grandpa? Pop. He'd have been a Pop for sure.

While Ted was going to be a dad.

A dad. A father. With a child. A child who would be entirely reliant on him. Him and Addy. Addy, who'd be the most amazing mother, of that he had no doubt.

It was himself he was struggling to picture. Likely because he'd put in great effort never to picture himself that way before.

Would he be like his own dad? His situation

was very different. He didn't live in a house with a library, or even a backyard. He wasn't even living with the child's mother. They'd known one another a couple of months, while his parents had been together a decade before he was born.

And his own father had died suddenly when Ted was nineteen. From a disease that still had no cure.

Ted pressed a fist to his chest, and said, "I can picture you looking at me, one eyebrow raised, waiting for me to explain myself. 'Be careful with girls,' you'd said when you sat me down for the talk. 'Be respectful. And take responsibility.' And I have. Always. This…this was…"

A broken condom. Damaged condom. Out of date condom. Overly hasty putting on of condom. Destiny?

"Unplanned." A beat, and, "Which I'm sure you've picked up on over the years. If you've been listening at all. So, I'm not telling Mum yet, okay?"

Not till it felt more real. Not till, medically, it was more…safe. Till then it was only a possibility. No need for his mother to invest. Emotionally. Not fully. Not yet.

It was early days. And things could change. He knew he was thinking twelve steps ahead of where he ought, but contingencies, playing out eventualities, risk assessment, was his life. It was ingrained.

Things could go wrong.

He knew, from the maternity rotation he'd done at uni, that the first three months were fraught with danger for the embryo.

Then there was concern for the mother. Look at him. He'd broken the mould. A saying that he'd never fully appreciated till he imagined Adelaid in his mother's place.

Flicking fingers to get blood back into his extremities, he moved on. Once born there were choking hazards, broken bones, unforeseen congenital issues. How any parent made it through without developing stress ulcers was beyond his understanding.

In fact, if "pregnancy" came past his desk, seeking funding, he would pass. Far too many variables, so few of them positive.

Pressing himself from the couch so that he might pace the room, his gaze caught on the small yellow pot on the windowsill. Fuzz Lightyear, the quaint little cactus Adelaid had given him. The only furnishing, apart from his dad's chair, he'd ever brought into this room.

Ask him three months earlier if he'd have a cactus, name a cactus, care about a cactus, and he'd have thought you were crazy. But here he was. In a different mental and emotional place than he had been for a very long time.

Because of Adelaid.

He saw the world differently now. Not as mere science, as fact and fiction. But messy, and adventurous, and varied, and in full technicolour. So much so he'd begun to open himself up to the possibility of a future with her. Her strength and determination not a distraction from his mission, but an elevation of his life.

From the moment he'd seen her she'd been inevitable.

Fingers spinning his father's watch around and around and around on his wrist, he said. "You'd like her, Dad. Strike that, you'd love her. I can so imagine the two of you bonding over Hitchcock movies, Mum and I watching from the sidelines, shaking our heads. She's marvellous, Dad. Tender. Hopeful and loyal. She opens her arms to people, even those who might hurt her, which terrifies me. She's—she's the one."

Only his dad didn't respond. For his dad wasn't really there. And never would be again.

Which was why Ted's entire existence had been built on discipline. On rigorously tested fact. While Adelaid's was built on hope. She'd rubbed off on him, for sure.

But was it enough?

Enough was enough. He couldn't continue mulling, hypothesising, talking to his dead father, while Adelaid was out there, no doubt feeling as confused, and shocked, and daunted, as he was.

Work could wait. The time to go to her was now.

* * *

Adelaid opened the door to find Ted on her porch once again. Only this time he didn't ask to come in. This time he stepped over the threshold and swept her up in his arms.

And soon they were kissing, and clawing at one another's clothes, as if their very lives depended on it.

"Wait." It was Ted that time, drawing back. "I came here to talk."

"Yes. We should talk."

With a growl, he kissed her again. Kept kissing her as he walked her into the lounge room. And there he put her down carefully, gently, as if suddenly aware how small she was compared to him.

Adelaid sat on one end of the couch and patted the seat beside her. "You look like you're about to pass out. Or throw up. I have dibs, for the next few weeks at least."

Ted sat, a kind of psychic pain flashing over his face.

"I'm joking," she said. "I feel fine. How about you?"

He blanked her, but his mouth kicked up at one corner.

Then she said, "It's yours by the way. The baby."

His expression was priceless. Momentarily baffled, before he burst into laughter. "Hell, Addy. I can safely say I wasn't expecting to laugh like that today."

She reached out and took his hand, moving it into her lap. "I've had a few laugh-or-cry moments myself. This is huge. And unforeseen. And no one's fault. I told you I wasn't on the pill, right? But we used condoms. So—"

He lifted her hand and laid a kiss to the palm, and her nerves seemed to unknot, all over her body.

"Science," said Ted, "is often fallible. How do you feel? Honestly."

"Tired. Queasy. Sideswiped." A beat, then, "Scared."

"Of...motherhood?" The word sat strangely on his tongue. As if he'd have gone with a more scientific term if he hadn't forced himself to be real. Adelaid decided to ignore the red flag. Focussing instead on the fact that he was there, holding her hand.

Adelaid shook her head. "A dozen nieces and nephews. Three sisters-in-law to call on for advice when, or if, I feel the need. I've got this." Her eyes rose to meet his. "I'm scared of everything that must be going on in your head right now."

His expression, the way he was clearly trying to appear strong, and supportive and fine, near broke her heart. For it was clear as day to her that he was holding on by his fingernails. She shoved red flag number two deep down inside.

"I know you don't want kids, Ted. Or a family. You made that very clear. But you need to know that I... I feel very strongly about going ahead with the pregnancy. For many reasons. Yes, it's unplanned. And yes, I'd prefer to be in a more stable position than I am right now." A job with health insurance would have been nice. "But it's real. And happening. And growing. And I was unplanned. And I'm pretty bloody happy to be here. So…"

Ted shook his head. "If you harboured any thought that I'd ask you to not… Addy, that was never going to happen."

She knew it. But boy did it feel good to hear it. "Thank you. For saying that. Now I also understand if you… If you can't…"

Ted moved closer, slid his big strong sure hand into the hair behind her neck and said, "I didn't want a cactus. But you should see Fuzz Lightyear now."

That's all it took for tears that had been hiding away inside of her to spill from her eyes like salty waterfalls. "What are you saying?"

"I'm saying," he said slowly, "that we go on as we have been going on. With forward momentum. One step at a time. One kiss at a time. One bombshell at a time."

She swiped at her tears, laughter falling from her mouth. "It's a crazy thought, right? You are never home, my hours are all over the place. You're a neat freak, I'm a mess. You're always on time, I'm always late. I'm static electricity, you're Mr Cool." She flapped a hand at him, sitting there, proving it.

"We're both pretty determined people, Addy."

He was giving her everything she could hope for, in the situation. And yet, something ate at her. Some third red flag that she couldn't put her finger on. "How are you so calm about this?"

Ted breathed out hard, his hand finally rubbing up the back in his neck in that way she loved so much. "I'm not calm. I'm jumbled and overthinking things and shell-shocked, actually. And I may have spent a good bit of time earlier today talking to my father's ghost." He shook his head. "I just... I don't want to lose this. I don't want to lose you."

"Oh, Ted," she said, before crawling along the couch and into his arms. And whether it was raging hormones, or just simply Ted, she had to have him. Had to show him, with action, what she could not find the words to say.

That she had no clue what she'd done to deserve him, but she'd do whatever it took not to lose him too.

Her hands on his face she drew him to her and kissed him. Hard. Not holding back an ounce of her feelings. This was big, and raw, and scary, but she had Ted, and he was holding her, and he had belief in her. Belief in *them*.

And that was far more than she'd ever had in her life. More than she'd ever dared hope for, in her wildest dreams.

Kisses not letting up, she straddled him, her body sinking over his thighs. Rocking into him as his hands roved down her back before landing on her backside, holding her to him. His tongue slid into her mouth as he rocked up into her, the actions mimicking what was to come.

"Is this okay?" he murmured against her moth.

"I'm pregnant, Ted, not infirmed."

He pulled away, just long enough to swipe her hair from her face and run his thumb down her cheek. And with that he rolled her onto the couch, holding his bulk over her. His eyes dark, and hot, and possessive, he stripped her.

And then, after she asked it of him, he was inside her. Bare. Skin on skin. All slippery heat and gasping sighs.

For a brief spell, there was nothing between them but sweat and breath. No tension, no fear, no uncertainty about what the future might bring.

And afterwards, as they lay snuggled on her couch, Ted caressing her hair from her face, while reading articles on pregnancy on his phone, tossing her little nuggets such as when it was best to tell people, and why folate was important, she didn't have it in her to tell him she was all over it.

She'd remind him she didn't need looking after later. Right now, after the day she'd had, it felt like the nicest thing in the world.

And so things went for the next fortnight.

They'd agreed to tell their closest friends the news, mostly so that they each had someone to click fingers in front of their faces if they disppeared into their own heads too often. Georgette took up knitting "so the kid would have warm feet." Hadley shook her head every time she saw Ted, and Ronan was avoiding him. Forward momentum indeed.

Till one morning, while nursing her morning espresso, Celia introduced Ted to every second person who entered the tennis club, leaving Ted to realise *he* ought to have chosen the venue for their coffee.

"Now," Celia said when she noticed Ted checking his watch for the third time, "what's new with you?"

"I wanted to talk to you about something… personal."

Celia's hand went to her throat. "Darling?"

Ted grimaced, wondering whether either of them would be able to do or say anything out of the normal without their minds going straight to bloody cancer.

"I'm fine. I just wanted to ask you something. If you wouldn't mind telling me what exactly happened when I *broke the mould.*"

Celia blinked. "Well, that's rather unexpected. But all right. It was a rare complication. You were a Caesarean birth. A blood vessel was nicked just as the doctor was stitching me up. Nobody knew until my blood pressure dropped dramatically several hours later, my insides filling with blood.

It was all rather dire, according to your father, but I remember none of it. A couple of operations and lots of transfusions later and and here we are."

Ted was not squeamish. Medical research was a rather earthy field. Yet he felt his own blood pressure take a dip.

"Is there a particular reason you're asking? Some project you're working on your dear old mum could help with?"

Here goes, thought Ted, readying to say words he'd honestly never expected would come out of his mouth.

"I'm pregnant."

Celia gasped, a shaky hand going to her mouth.

Ted ran a hand over his face to find his forehead had broken out in a sweat. "Well, not me. Adelaid. Whom you met. Adelaid Adams, the writer. We weren't involved when you met her, but have become so. And Adelaid is pregnant. And the… It is mine."

"Ted," she said, so many emotions flashing behind her eyes he could not hope to keep up. "Oh, Ted. I am so happy for you both. Does she know you're here? Telling me?"

"She knows. She's telling her own family now too." He'd wanted to be with her, but she'd insisted it was something she had to do on her own. A rather strong surge in her need for independence a definite side effect of her pregnancy.

"And does she know you're worried about her?"

Ted sat back. "I'm not worried. You're referring to my query? I'm collecting knowledge so as to be prepared for any eventuality."

"Darling, that is the definition of worry. Here's the only piece of unsolicited parenting advice you will get from me. Ignorance really is bliss."

Ted's jaw ticked as he ground his teeth. "That seems counterintuitive."

She smiled. "I feel for your generation with your social media groups and your how-to podcasts. There is such a thing as too much information. For a man such as yourself, your retention capabilities, I'm not sure how you sleep at night."

He didn't for the most part. Then Adelaid had come along, and something about knowing she was out there in the world had settled him. But since she'd fallen pregnant, he was back to his old ways. There were only a few months for him to prepare.

Ted said, "I just want to make sure there's nothing in particular I ought to mention to the OBGYN, regarding your situation."

"You are most welcome to tell him, or her, to take care with their scalpels, but if that's something you feel you need to bring up, then perhaps you ought to choose a different OBGYN."

Celia placed her hand over his. "I know this is like telling the moon not to pull the tides, but stop trying to control it all, Ted. It's simply not possible. Take care of her. Encourage her to rest when she can, to eat well and drink plenty of water. Get some fresh air and sunshine." Celia shrugged. "For all the wonder of science, the basics have never really changed."

Celia clicked her fingers and asked for a menu. Then passed it to Ted.

"Now order something, darling, before you pass out. And you let me know when I am allowed to spoil you all rotten, all right?"

"All right."

The Adams family chat went something like this.

Adelaid: Up the duff. Ted's the dad. Can't make Sunday lunch this week.

Three seconds later.

Brad: Where are you?

Adelaid: Home.

Brad: Don't move. We'll be right there.

Adelaid sat on the front porch, eating corn chips dipped in cream cheese, and watched as three separate utes pulled up outside, one after the other. She pulled herself to standing, braced her feet against the floor, crossed her arms and waited for the onslaught.

Sid, the youngest, and his girlfriend Sally — no kids yet—made it up the path first and held out a fist.

"Is that for me to—?"

He slammed his fist into hers. "Bouya!"

Jake was next. He pulled her in for a manly hug, double back-slap. "Way to lock that down, kid."

"What is happening here?"

Brad was last, as he was unwinding a tarp from the back of his ute, and pulling out what looked like several pieces of hand-me-down baby furniture.

"Stop!" she called, and he stopped. "Can you leave all that for a second and come inside?"

Brad slowly put the high chair back into the tray, then ambled up the path. "What are you wearing?"

Adelaid looked down. "Georgette's overalls. I'm not loving the feel of things touching my stomach right now. Because I'm pregnant."

Nope. Nothing.

Except, "Is he here?"

"If by 'he' you mean Ted, then no, he's having breakfast with his mother, then he has a video link-up with the UN about some freshwater project Big Think are close to launching."

A grunt. Then Brad followed the others inside, noses lifted to follow the scent of fresh baked muffins in the kitchen.

Couching and spluttering at the sky, which

looked serenely back, Adelaid headed in. "Where's Bill?"

"First responder to a four-car pile-up on the M1. He sends his congratulations."

"So you did all actually read my message. Telling you that I am pregnant. While unmarried. Having recently quit my well-paying job."

Again she braced herself, waiting for the fall-out. The opinions. The comparison to their mum.

"We like him," said Sid, a mouthful of muffin.

"He's bloody clever," said Jake. "And rich. *BRW Rich List*–level rich. We looked him up."

Brad leant back, muffin in hand, a delighted smile on his face.

A frisson of something that felt awfully like envy skittered down her spine. "What does any of that have to do with this?"

One of them frowned. Or maybe they all did. They'd clearly—as they so often did—become a single wall of opinionated muscle.

"What's with the sass?" asked Jake. "You tell us all the time that we need to stop telling you what to do, that you're a grown-up, that you can make your own choices. We're trying to say you've done good."

Adelaid's mouth popped open. Literally. Her jaw dropping with a clunk.

Her voice was raw as she said, "So let me get this straight. You're finally happy to leave me be, to make my own choices, without butting your big noses in, because I brought home a big strong man who can do the job you guys have been doing my whole life?"

"That's gotta be a relief, right?" said Jake. "It is to us."

Adelaid stalked over and snatched up the tray of muffins, which got their attention.

"Addy, come on—"

"I have been 'doing good' for years. I graduated high school, winning the principal's arts award, despite barely attending primary. Graduated university, while holding down two jobs. In a highly competitive industry, I hustled my way into a lucrative position with a thrillingly popular digital media company. I have enough money for a deposit on a house. And I've kept a cactus alive for seven months now. I am also growing a life inside of me, which is more than any of you have ever done."

Breathing heavily, blood rising, she said, "I was sure you'd all barrel over here and give me what for, for being single, and pregnant. Like Mum."

"You're not single."

"I am, for all intents and purposes."

Brad frowned, but kept his counsel for once.

Jake scoffed. "And you're not Mum."

Adelaid's gaze whipped to Jake. "What does that mean?"

"She was sick, Ads. Some way, somehow. Mentally, physically, who knows. We tried to get her to see a doctor to find out why. But we were too young to know what else to do. When she died... well, we didn't want to make that same mistake twice. So yeah, maybe we've been on your case. We also made sure you had the best doctors, and therapists, and Brad was onto your high school weekly, making sure they knew how lucky they were to have you."

Brad's jaw ticked. "We know how much you adored her. We didn't want to mar that memory. But just so you know, we've never been concerned that you were like her. In anything but the good bits."

Sid was nearest, so she grabbed him and hugged him like crazy. Then waggled a hand till the others joined them. "Thank you."

"Now can we have another muffin?" asked Sid, his voice muffled.

"Did I have to withhold food? Is that really all I had to do to get you guys to listen? And talk to me?"

Adelaid gave them each a bag of muffins and sent them on their way.

"Can I bring in the baby gear now?" Brad asked. "Betty has had it sitting in the garage for like a fortnight."

"No," said Adelaid. "If I want your help, I'll ask for it. I promise."

Brad sighed, then they were gone. Leaving

Adelaid feeling light-headed, flabbergasted and strangely bereft.

She found her phone, then sent Ted a message, telling him she was done. And giving him a quick recap. Then she slumped onto a stool in the kitchen and ate muffin crumbs from the cutting board.

Forward momentum had been wondrous. Her brothers might actually have just washed their hands of her. And Ted... Ted was out there telling his mother that he was going to be a father. All it would take for her life to be pretty much perfect right now was for someone to call and offer to buy her story.

Her feet felt a little numb. Her fingertips lacked sensation. And she found herself having to breathe. Deep settling breaths.

What was a person to do, if after having to fight for everything they ever wanted, one day they looked up and found they had it all?

Later that day, still feeling not quite herself, Adelaid alighted her ride share, kicking at the hemline of the floaty seventies maxidress she'd borrowed from Georgette, as she could no longer stand the feel of anything tight over her tummy so that she didn't trip over the thing.

About to meet with a book club who'd collected over a hundred thousand dollars' worth o book donations for a flooded library, Adelaid's phone buzzed.

"Hello?" she answered, while tugging at the collar of the dress, which had twisted up in her shoulder bags.

"You, my darling girl, are a genius."

"Deborah?" Her old editor. "Hi! So nice to hear from you! And why am I a genius?"

"Not sure if you heard, but I moved on too, after you left." Deborah went on to mention the name of a publication that made Adelaid's heart stop. "A sample of your Ted Fincher profile fell onto my desk today. What are the odds? I read it, I loved it. I've spoken to everyone here about the wonder that is you, and we'd love to publish your piece."

Adelaid's heart leapt into her throat so that for a second all she could do was squeak. Then, "Oh, my gosh. Deborah! Thank you!"

"We'd also love you to come in and chat about what's next."

Adelaid moved off the footpath when a teacher with a group of kindergarteners all holding a rope wandered up the path. "Of course," she said, watching the little ones wobble and bounce and spin. "I would love that."

"Now," said Deborah, her voice quieting, "I shouldn't be saying this, but what with all the offers you must be weighing right now, go with your gut, push for what you want. Know your worth."

Other offers? *Ha. Ha-ha-ha-ha.* Adelaid said, "You bet. Great advice."

"Then after you do all that, choose us. It would be wonderful to have you on board again."

With that Deborah rang off.

Adelaid's phone began to buzz.

"Ms Adams."

Adelaid tucked her phone between ear and shoulder and rejigged her bags. "This is she."

"This is Daryl Majors from *Imprint*. I've read your Big Think piece and believe its place is right here. With us."

"Thank you so much! That's so nice to hear."

Giving up on her bags, she dumped the lot of them on the verge, and shuffled through her tote till she found paper and pen. Writing down *Deborah* and then *Daryl... Imprint.*

"Any requests—word length, tone, etc.?" she asked.

"We loved it."

"Every word?" she joked.

After a pause, he said, "Every word."

Her pen hovered over the paper.

"I've emailed you a contract. Sign it, send it back and we'll release the funds immediately."

Wow. That was...fast. "I'll have a look and get back to you."

Feeling a tingle up the back of her neck, Adelaid opened her email on her phone to find no less than five more offers for her story.

Seven altogether. So why wasn't she jumping for joy?

Partly because the same dress felt weird, and airy and not at all her. But also, seven offers? After weeks of nothing?

It was a dream. The kind of dream in which you know you are dreaming because it was way too unreal.

She lifted her phone and called Deborah back.

Ted leaned against the picket fence outside the converted weatherboard dwelling in which their OBGYN resided, watching the street for Adelaid's Uber, and unconsciously twisting his watch around his wrist.

Dr Shifarko had a waiting list a mile long, but she had also been an early sensitivity consultant on stem cell research for Big Think, so a quick text and he'd had an appointment that day. Adelaid wasn't the only one who had a fondness for "connections."

Adelaid. Who was late. For their first scan.

It was still early days, so there might not be answers as yet, as to whether the pregnancy was tracking as it ought.

Not that he was *concerned*.

Yes, he felt a low-level discomfort in his gut. But it was the same thing that had driven him all these years. How could he not be feeling something, when according the World Health Organisation nearly a thousand women a day died from preventable causes related to childbirth and pregnancy.

Not that he was *worried*.

Skilled care, before, during and after was key, hence the choice of OBGYN. Despite his mother's advice, Ted believed himself prepared for any eventuality. It was his job to look out for those he cared for.

Speaking of people he cared for, where the hell was Adelaid?

Her habitual lateness was a symptom of her condition. He understood that. But today of all days?

Foot tapping on the path, Ted went to check the time, twisting his dad's watch, only the clasp was unbuckled and it slipped over his hand, landing facedown on the footpath with a dull thud.

Time hung for a second, two, three, before Ted leaned over to pick up the watch. To find a crack had split the face in two. He swiped the pad of his thumb over the face, a sliver of glass cutting into his thumb. The low-level discomfort in his belly rising to a solid medium.

He was sucking his thumb still when a car pulled up and Adelaid barrelled out, a voluminous flowery dress billowing around her, a thousand bags over her shoulder, her hair a wild mass of curls floating about her face.

His heart fair stopped at the sight of her. It hovered in his chest a good three seconds before kicking like a mule and keeping him alive once more.

And it hit him, like a sledgehammer to the head—no matter what happened in the scan, whether a second heart beat inside of her or no, he wasn't going anywhere.

Adelaid was the one.

"Did you tell them to do it?" she asked, descending on him with rather a lot of energy, even for her.

Ted dragged himself out of his fog of adoration, to find he was still sucking his thumb. Pulling it from his mouth, he directed her towards the doctor's gate, and began walking that way. "Let's head in, yes? And did I tell whom to do what?"

When she didn't move, bar shifting her bags from one shoulder to the other, he went to her, reaching for the straps. Only to stop when she held up both hands, arms straight, eyes wild, halting him where he stood.

"Did you," she said, through gritted teeth, "or did you not call my dream editors with regards to my profile piece, and somehow make it sound as if it was worth their while to offer me the moon?"

"What on earth are you ta—" Something tugged in the back of Ted's mind. A sense of warning, of imminent danger, had him pulling up straight.

Noting his hesitation, she moved closer. Green

wildfire flickering behind her gaze. Then growling, she tugged at the dress, some hippie number that made her look like she was about to sport a peace sign. While everything else about her screamed war.

A responding growl built up in his chest. And, doctor's appointment be damned, he'd have dragged her behind the nearest bush if not for the fact there was no denying she was furious. With him.

"Ted," she said, her voice danger soft. "Promise me no editors were coerced into bidding on my story."

"*Coerced* is a strong word."

"I knew it!" She began to pace, muttering under her breath about everyone going whacka-doo, when she was the one who was meant to be hormonal.

He wasn't keen on the pink in her cheeks. The rise and fall of her chest. The signs that her heart rate was up. Yes, she suffered a hyperactivity disorder that could bring on such symptoms. But assuming his father was losing weight on purpose had been the death of him, literally.

Ted shook his head. Correlation, not causation. Conflating one thing with another was not going to help. Still, he didn't need to be an obstetric specialist to know stress was not a good thing in the first trimester.

He held out both hands, attempting to stay her. "Settle, sweetheart. Just settle."

She stopped pacing. "Did you really just tell me to *settle*?"

"It was a suggestion. Medically motivated. Can we discuss this afterward?" Ted went to check his watch, then remembered it was in his hand. Broken. He slipped it into his pocket.

While Adelaid shook her head. "I'd had no other offers on the profile. Not a sniff. I'd hoped that my work would speak for itself."

"It will. It does. You are a wonderful writer."

"I know! While you're about to become the thinking woman's muffin overnight."

"What about the *unthinking* women?" He held up a hand the moment he said it. "I did not intend to make light. I only want to do what it takes to get you through that door, so that we can find out if… If the pregnancy is even viable."

She glanced up at the beautiful old building, the oak trees, dappled sunshine. Her throat working. Her hand lifting to land on her belly.

The urge to go to her, to lay his hand over hers, was primal. But something held him back. Some final layer of self-protection, bolstered by the broken watch in his pocket, the unsettling conversation with his mother and finally Adelaid refusing to play ball when it came to her safety.

Too many variables.

Yet he added one more. "Ronan would not have

been wrong in knowing how much I want to see you rewarded for all your hard work."

He saw the light flare in her eyes, then dim, before she breathed out, long and slow, her chin falling to her chest. "Ted."

Birds twittered in the trees overhanging the avenue. A light breeze rustled the light layer of fallen leaves. Ted could feel her drawing away from him as if it was a physical thing.

She said, "Can you even imagine how mortifying it was, hearing words of praise from the mouths of people I would give my right foot to impress, while suspecting that they'd been nudged into it. What will they think when it comes out that I am your…?"

She flicked a heavy hand his way, unwilling or still unable to put a label on what they were.

While Ted could think of a dozen. She was his confidante, his friend, his lover, his joy. She was the person he wanted to wake up next to for the rest of his life. *She was the one.*

"They'll think you are a talented writer with connections. How do you think we got so big so fast? We've used every connection we made. Because we believed that what we had to offer had worth. Use me. Lean on me. I will get no greater pleasure than using my influence to help you in any way that I can."

Adelaid swallowed, and he hoped like hell she could see his intentions had been true.

Till she said, "It just feels wrong. Everything feels wrong. These clothes feel wrong. The way my brothers just accepted this as fait accompli, then dropped me like a hot potato, that was so wrong. I liked my life. I liked my hustle. I liked the fact that I was at a point where I put less store in how other people saw me as I'd learned to like myself. Now everything is changing so fast I don't recognise myself anymore."

"Adelaid, that's not—"

"*Fair?* Tell me about it. Some people are born into happy families, some are born into struggle. Some people are given respect from day dot, others leave first impressions they can never break, no matter how hard they try. But despite all that, you can't wrap me in cotton wool, Ted."

A muscle jumped in Ted's cheek. He'd thought he'd imagined all the ways this could go wrong. It seemed he'd missed quite a lot.

"I'd really appreciate it if you'd let me try."

She laughed, but there was no humour in it. In fact, a single tear wavered down her cheek. "I get it. You fix things. You make them better. Because of your dad. It is a noble pursuit. But I'm not one of your causes, Ted. I don't need fixing."

He opened his mouth to deny her claim, then remembered his mother's prophetic reminder that he couldn't possibly control it all.

Letting go a big deep breath, Adelaid reached into her bag, pulled out her phone and dialled.

Hand shaking a little she held it to her ear, a watery smile plastered on her face as she said, "Daryl, hi, it's Adelaid Adams. Unfortunately, I'm going to have to pull my piece from contention." Top teeth biting down on her bottom lip as if to stop it from trembling, she listened. Nodded. "Thank you, truly. I'll absolutely be in touch when I have something else lined up. So be prepared!"

When she made the next call, Ted wanted to grab her phone, to stop her from sabotaging herself in that way. But she'd literally just spent the past several minutes making it clear that her sense of self-determination was at stake.

Meaning, Ted had to stand there, feeling impotent and ineffective, as she made call after call. Watching the woman he loved feel pain, in real time, and knowing there was nothing he could do about it, hurt like a bastard.

"What's the time?" she said when she was done. Then, "Where's your watch?"

He pulled it from his pocket and passed it to her.

She took it, saw the break, her face crumpling. "Oh, Ted." Then, "Come on. Let's go inside now. You're right, we'll figure out the rest after."

"I don't want—" he said, his voice croaking. "I want—"

You. I want you. And us. And this...

But most of all he wanted Adelaid to be happy. To feel strong, and fierce, and bright, and proud.

To own the space she'd worked so hard to carve out for herself. If he crushed that, if he crushed all the things he loved most about her, he'd never be able to live with himself.

"Dr Shifarko comes highly recommended, but if you want to see someone else, then we find someone else." Too little, too late. "Might I suggest we take this appointment so we can be sure that you are okay?"

Only as Adelaid looked to him, her eyes bruised, did he realise the hum inside of him, that was now ratcheted up as high as he'd ever felt it go, had nothing to do his being a scientist. And everything to do with him being a man.

A man pretending he wasn't deeply daunted by the entire situation. By the terrifying flipside that came with feeling so much. A man forced to look into the face of his own intrinsically hard-wired flaws and not know how to fix himself.

Adelaid tipped the broken hardware into his palm. Then, fixing the straps of her bags, she moved through the gate and said, "Come on, then. Let's get this over with."

And so, they walked into the doctor's office, side by side. The gulf between them interminable.

CHAPTER NINE

"HEY," SAID GEORGETTE, head poking out of the kitchen doorway. "Deborah called. Twice. Sounded super keen to talk to you. You're home early. Thought you'd be off making lovey eyes at your beautiful beast, and— Hey what's wrong?"

Adelaid's bags slumped to the floor by the front door.

"Oh, no," said Georgette, jogging down the hall. "The baby—?"

"Has a heartbeat," said Adelaid with a quivering smile. "A beautiful, perfect, teeny tiny little heartbeat."

Georgette's hands went to her mouth. "Then what am I missing? Is it Ted? Does Ted not have a heartbeat? I knew it. He's a vampire. Or from Krypton or something. No man that big and that beautiful is real."

Adelaid trudged into the lounge, and slumped facedown on the couch. Then remembered what she and Ted had done on that couch. Then remembered she didn't like things touching her stomach. So she pressed her sorry self up to sitting.

"Deborah was calling to offer to buy my story."

"Woohoo! When it rains it pours!"

Adelaid slowly sat forward till her face fell into her hands. "Only because Ted, or Ronan on Ted's behalf, or Hadley on Ronan's behalf on Ted's behalf, put out word around town that anyone who bought my story would be looked on kindly by Big Think. Or something of that ilk."

"Wow!" said Georgette. Then, "That's massive! They're notoriously tight. They don't show favour to anyone, making our job much more difficult. Only...you look like that's a bad thing."

"It is a bad thing! He thought I couldn't do it on my own."

"Ronan?"

"Ted!"

"What? That doesn't sound at all like him. I've seen him read your own stories back to you, he loves them so much."

Well, no, it didn't sound like Ted.

But then again neither had the fact that he'd made her feel powerless.

When she would not, could not, be reliant on anyone. Her brothers, being men, didn't understand how much she feared ending up in the position her mother had. Left behind, overwhelmed by circumstance.

"Look at it this way," said Georgette. "You got

your foot in the door with Big Think because of me. Did you feel bad about that?"

Adelaid blinked. "No."

"Because you know I know you're amazing, or because you know I helped you because I love you. Or both."

Adelaid let that sink in.

"As for Ted," said Georgette, "the man's hardly oblivious. The only reason he would have stepped over some invisible line you'd created in your head is because you invited him over that line. In fact, that man would take down the stars, one by one, and place them in your hands, if you asked it of him. Or even if he thought it would make you happy. That's how opposite of oblivious he is."

Georgette tapped her lips.

Adelaid wriggled on the seat. "Do you really think—"

"Stay there. I'm going to bring you a snack. Need to keep your blood sugar up!"

"Not sure that's right," said Adelaid, remembering something Dr Shifarko had said about gestational diabetes.

But Georgette was gone. Leaving Adelaid alone, feeling lost and yearning for starlight.

She grabbed a fluffy orange cushion with big knobbly pom-poms lining the edges and held it to her stomach. Georgette thought it the most uncomfortable thing on the planet. Ted, when it had ended up under his back one time, had yanked it out from under himself, looked at it, then looked at her as if to say, *What on earth is this?*

"It makes me happy," she'd said.

And after showering her with his killer smile, he'd placed it gently on the coffee table as if it was something precious. Purely because it had meaning to her.

"He likes to take care of me." Saying the words out loud, without tone or censure, they sounded like a dream.

When she thought about it, she liked to take care of him too. Keeping food on hand for when he forgot to eat. Gently forcing him to look up from his work. All the ways she'd imposed herself on him, on his sense of order, because she'd seen a need in him. And sought to fill it.

Only he hadn't complained or refused her. He'd made room. He'd let her in. He'd appreciated her inclinations. Her ways of showing him that she…

That she loved him.

She loved Ted. She loved him so much she had no clue where to put it all.

Her love was an inevitable tumble into his warmth, and generosity and wonderfulness. Until, now she thought of it, she couldn't remember a moment of having known him when she hadn't loved him.

Was that what he'd been doing for her, making appointments on her behalf with fancy doctors, giving her career a leg up? Helping carry her bags, because he saw that she was walking funny. Swiping her hair from her face, as if he knew the texture of it would eventually drive her nuts. Showing her that he thought her amazing. Showing her that he loved her. Only in his far more worldly way?

Ted, who'd been cradling his father's broken watch when she'd come at him, a whirling dervish of referred pain, with nowhere to put it now that her Teflon brothers had left her be.

Ted, who'd been shifting from foot to foot, anxious to get her inside to the doctor. Not because of some appointment he'd made on her behalf, but because he'd suffered loss in his life, and wanted to make sure *she* was okay.

Ted, whose face she'd watched for a full minute when the baby's heartbeat was found. Every last twitch inside of her had settled as she'd drunk in the wonder, the delight, and the relief in his expression. Before his eyes had swung to hers, a glint of actual tears therein.

She reached into one of the pockets in her borrowed dress, and pulled out the picture from the sonogram. Nothing but a tiny dark smudge with a tiny white dot in the middle. Running a thumb a millimetre above the image, she thought, *No. nothing. Something. Everything.*

Before Ted her life was fine. Fine if you enjoy paddling a melting iceberg adrift in a warm sea

Since Ted her life had been a billion times better than fine.

On cue, her phone pinged.

Ted: Checking you made it home all right.

Adelaid: I did. Thank you.

Ted: Good.

Ted: Heads-up, I'll check in again tomorrow. And the next day. And the next. Unless you tell me not to.

Adelaid: Of course.

Ted: Till then.

Adelaid waited in case there was more. But it was just enough. Ted, not pressing, only making it clear he wasn't going anywhere. No matter how many emotional grenades she lobbed.

If she could get over herself, he was there for the having. It was all there, for the having. A home, a career, a family. A man who adored her, and believed in her, and loved her for all her quirks not despite them.

Adelaid buried her face in the cushion and screamed.

"Whoa! What did I miss?"

"He loves me."

Georgette blinked. "Between me leaving to get snacks and coming back…"

"I figured stuff out."

Georgette sat, the tray leaning precariously on her lap. And Adelaid handed over the sonogram image.

"Oh, sweet pea. It's a bean. You're growing a bean."

"Ted and I are growing a bean. Together." She could only hope it wasn't too late to let Ted know it.

Ronan stormed into the Batcave, waving his phone in Ted's direction.

Ted looked up from the black-and-white sonogram image he held in his hand, his brain feeling like lead wrapped in tinfoil. "You got my email."

"Hell, yes, I got your email. What's that?"

Ted held up the sonogram.

Ronan looked at it for a full three seconds, before asking, "All well?"

"We have a heartbeat."

"Hell of a thing. Now what the hell's with the email? Couldn't walk into my office and say something to my face?"

Ted lifted himself out of his chair, blinked away the grit in his eyes and said, "I'll say it now, then. I'm taking a break."

"For how long?"

"A day. A week. Indefinitely."

"Ted. Come on. This is ridiculous—"

"She pulled the piece."

Ronan jerked, uncharacteristically taken aback. "What do you mean—?"

"She received several offers for her story today. Good money. Next looks. Everything she's been working towards. And she pulled it."

"Why?"

"Because you called a half-dozen editors and told them to make her an offer!" Ted's voice echoed back at him.

"Does that sound like something I would condescend to do?"

"Don't prevaricate. I know you did something."

Ronan's jaw released. "Our PR people were prepared for any calls looking for comment. They were given instruction to say that 'We at Big Think have always been committed to partnering with local talent,' and that I thought it a 'warm, humorous, impressively in-depth, well-balanced piece.'"

"Ronan—"

"You intimated that it was important to you that she—"

"I know!" said Ted, throwing out his arm and knocking over a cup filled with pencils. He watched them roll all over the place, a couple tumbling over the edge. And didn't feel the slightest urge to tidy them up. "I know."

He'd apprised Ronan of the situation, somewhat. His concern for her stress levels. His wish that more people got to hear her voice. And they'd known one another too long to pretend Ted hadn't known what Ronan would do.

"If it helps any," said Ronan, eyes serious, and curious, "not a word of our statement was untrue. As features go, it was well above par."

"You read it."

Ronan nodded, a slight smile tugging at his mouth. "She pinned you, like a moth to a board."

Ted lifted his hand, the back of his neck itching, but let it drop before he connected. "She has integrity. She worked really hard to get that chance. To get to know me. To write something lyrical, and beautiful, and moving, and quirky, and fresh and true. And now…now she feels as if, by blustering in and stamping ourselves all over it, we took that away from her."

"I refuse your request."

"My—"

"Your request for time off."

"So we're back to that. It wasn't a request. It's a done deal. I've put measures in place, provided Hadley with names, people who will step up. Who already have."

For he'd been stepping back, incrementally, in order to spend more time with Adelaid, and the world hadn't crumbled in his absence. In fact, he was clearer of the head. Actually more efficient, with sleep, good food, fresh air, sunshine and someone taking care of him.

Who knew?

"Are you listening to yourself?" said Ronan. "You do not take time off, Ted. You haven't had a holiday in ever. Ever since this girl came along—"

Ted was on his feet, his hands were fisted in the front of Ronan's shirt before he even felt himself move. Nostrils flared, adrenaline scented the air. And it took every ounce of restraint Ted could gather not to shove his friend against nearest wall.

"Her name," said Ted, "is Adelaid."

Ronan smiled. The bastard actually smiled. "I know her name, mate. I was just checking that you remembered it too."

What the—?

"This entire conversation, you've not said it once. It's a thing you do when in the process of... disentangling yourself. Hence the fact I rarely bother to learn the names of the women you see. Saves time."

Ted uncurled his fingers, and asked, "Are you trying to be an asshole, or does it come naturally?"

"Both, I imagine," Ronan drawled. Then, "You are my friend. And if disentangling is your intention, I stand by you. But..." A rare falter as Ronan looked for the right words. "I have to admit, it would be a surprise. Adelaid Adams might not be the best thing that ever happened to you—for that would be me, Sawyer comes a distant third—but she's close. Since she came along it's been like watching Pinocchio becoming a real boy."

Fanciful words for Ronan Gerard, but Ted knew exactly what he meant.

"Maybe you should be the one to take a break."

"Whatever," said Ronan.

If what Adelaid wanted from him was space, then…

No. Space wasn't what Adelaid wanted. What she wanted was to be seen. And heard. And given the benefit of the doubt.

His work with Big Think was important, worth his best efforts and extremely fulfilling, but it wasn't his whole life. Not anymore.

"So what now?" Ronan asked, still there.

"You want to know how I plan to make it up to my girlfriend?"

"You apologise. Tell her she's right."

Ted didn't even pretend to disagree.

"You should know, PR were also ordered to let Adelaid know that if she's ever keen to write a profile on Sawyer, or…" a beat, then "…or me, then she has an open invitation. Whether you stuff the whole relationship thing up, or not."

As he left Ronan added, "I'll let you have a week. The other zillion weeks you're owed you can save for when the baby is born. You'll need it."

"Wasn't a request!" Ted called, hand cupped around his mouth. "Don't require your permission!"

Then laughed when Ronan said, "Whatever gets you through the night."

Ted sat back in the chair, letting the hydraulics float him about, his mind doing much the same. Then he wheeled the thing to a desk with a computer and pulled up Adelaid's piece.

Odd as it was, reading about himself, he did so again. Only this time, he imagined Adelaid reading it to him.

And as her words, her tone, her humour, her heart, flowed over him, he began to see it for what it really was. Not merely an artful, wry, clever telling of the story of a thirty-something billionaire science geek, it was a love letter. To him. For all the world to see.

It's not about me, Adelaid had said over and over again.

But it was all about her, and had been from the very beginning.

A Bee Gees song jiving through her earbuds, loose gingham dress swishing about her ankles, Adelaid marvelled at the façade of the Big Think Corp building and felt sick to the stomach.

She reached into her tote for a slice of lemon and gave it a quick lick. Both Betty and Wendy had found it the perfect foil for morning sickness and so far, it was doing the trick. She put the lemon back, beside the container containing the chocolate chip muffin she'd made that morning.

Her phone buzzed. Not the Adams family chat, for it had quieted right down, all but overnight. A wind of change having descended upon the lot of them.

A message from Deborah.

Check email. Sent you a lead on special interest piece. Up your alley. Want?

Deborah, who'd refused to accept the withdrawal of her story. Deborah, who'd recommended she get an agent and sell the bloody thing. Her sample now about to hit social media, before the whole piece went in their online and print magazines.

Adelaid sent off a quick thumbs-up emoji, then scrolled down to her last messages from Ted, sent that morning.

Ted: Sleep okay?

Adelaid: Not so much. I watched Calamity Jane.

Ted: Not a shade on Pillow Talk.

Adelaid: Wash your mouth out with soap.

Ted's reply was an angel emoji!

All but hearing his voice in her head, Adelaid made a beeline for the rotating glass doors. Onc through, she saw Hadley talking to the staff at reception. Hadley offered up a nod, then a glance to the glass-fronted staff lift making its way towards the lobby.

"Ted," Adelaid said, the name wafting past her lips on a heady breath when she caught sight of his dark auburn hair, light glinting off his glasses, the sheer size of him compared to the others in the lift.

Adelaid's hand went to her belly. To the teeny tiny smudge therein.

And Ted looked up, as if something had tugged at his subconscious.

Spotting her through the glass, his hand lifted as if he might punch his way through the glass. But self-preservation got the better of him and he waited for the lift to reach the ground floor before he pushed past the poor staffers and jogged across the foyer, his hands going straight to her upper arms as he looked deep into her eyes.

"Everything okay?" he said, the words rough on his tongue. "Is the baby okay?"

Adelaid nodded. Smiled. And whatever he saw in her eyes had him hauling her into his chest. One arm across her back, the other in her hair. And there they stood, simply holding one another for the longest time.

"Your smell," she said, half smiling against his hard chest.

"Hmm?" he said, giving her a little air.

Not too much. Just the perfect amount.

She breathed him in. "I was feeling queasy but then you came, and now I feel nothing. Well, not *nothing*." Another wholesome breath in. "You're better than any lemon slice."

"Thank you?" The words rumbled from his chest to hers.

"You're welcome," she said on a sigh. Had he always smelled this good? This lickable? Good chance. Or perhaps it was a pregnancy bonus. If so, she couldn't wait to see what else it had in store for her.

Adelaid pressed herself back just enough that she could see his whole face. To find his eyes, dark and warm and gorgeous, moved between hers.

"Assuming you did not come here to sniff me, is there a particular reason you are here?" His voice was low. Edging towards a growl. As if he might be high on being with her too.

Adelaid swallowed. For all that she could see how he cared for her, in his messages, even after her flight, in the way he held her even now, this was it. This was her chance to step fully into whatever space he'd made for her in his life, leaving her old defensive ways behind.

"I've come to apologise—"

"There is no need."

She held up a hand. "There is very much a need."

His nostrils flared, and he nodded.

"I was a mess the other day. A perfect storm of every worry I've had in my entire life seemed to wash over me at once. I put it down to so many changes, and wobbles, and— What's the word?"

"Variables."

She clicked her fingers. "Yes. That's exactly it. I was unfair. To you. My expectations impossible. I'm so sorry I put you through that. When all you were doing was being protective, and prepared. Being...you. Considering the hormonal swings, I can't promise there won't be more episodes, going forward. Let's say there will be, just to be on the safe side."

"Going forward?" he asked, his voice deepening, his gaze roving over her face, the hand on her back sliding a little deeper around her waist.

"If that's what you want."

"Is it what you want?"

"Ted," she said, *her* voice now turning raspy, as if it had caught whatever it was that was making his eyes go hot. "I want this. I want us. I want—"

He leaned in and touched his lips to hers. Not shutting her up. More like sealing her words as a promise between them.

"You," Ted rumbled against her mouth, finishing her sentence as if he'd taken the word from her lips and made it his. "Would you care to hear what I want?"

"Please," she said, the word half whisper.

"I want this," he said, his hand reaching up to tug on a lock of her hair. "And this." His fingers cupping her jaw, his thumb tugged at her bottom lip. "I want every last bit of you. Hormones, mood swings, the lot."

"Thank the gods," she said, her breath leaving her on a whoosh of laughter, "or this whole moment would have been mighty confusing."

She earned a killer smile for her efforts. But she wasn't yet done. She had to make sure he knew how serious she was. No more guesswork. No more stumbling around all her big new feelings.

"Ted," she said. Then, "Theodore Fincher. The truth is, I never saw you coming. So even while you saw me, and accepted me, I was so swept up in you I lost myself. Just a bit."

Ted's eyes flew back to hers.

She lifted her hand to his cheek, to the rasp of stubble along the hard jaw. "But I'm back now. Still a scrappy little fighter, and now a lover, and soon enough, Smudge's mum."

Ted's mouth kicked up at one side. "Smudge?"

She held a hand over her belly. Then reached out for his hand and laid it over the top.

"Smudge," he said, his fingers closing around her hand.

Then his hand slipped a smidge lower, his little finger dipping into one of the big pockets in the side of her dress. She could get used to this, all the same.

"Ted," she warned, realising he had no idea what his scent was doing to her pregnancy-addled hormones. "I think maybe we should take this conversation elsewhere."

"I own the joint," he said, leaning to nuzzle her neck. "I can order everyone out of the building. Just like that. But first it's my turn to apologise."

"Ted—"

"My turn."

Adelaid nodded.

"My work has been my focus for as long as I can remember. And you, more than most anyone, know why. Any time I have paused, taken a breather, I've spent every minute holding my breath, dreading something bad happening to someone I love."

"Ted," she said, her voice gentle, her expression firm.

"I know that I am not the fixer of all things. I know when bad things happen it's not my fault. But I am also aware of the rarefied position I hold, the exceptional confluence of events that have given me the opportunity to enact real change on the world. And for as long as I can remember, I believed that it was my duty to take advantage of every chance I was gifted."

She pressed in closer.

"Then you came along and it was like someone had turned on a light. You showed me I'm no good to anyone if I'm burnt out. If I don't live a life that reminds me what I've been working so hard for."

She may have made a sound. Something between a sob and a sigh. For he tucked her under his chin, his arms wrapped all the way around her.

"You told me, many times, that our getting to know one another wasn't about you. But, Adelaid, sweetheart, from the moment you walked into my office, it's all been about you. I love you, Adelaid. One 'e.' You are worth pausing for."

Adelaid threw her arms around his neck, dragged him down to her level and kissed him. She kissed him till her head spun. She kissed him till she heard applause.

Ted lifted her, bodily, and spun her on the spot. And over his shoulder she could see faces galore looking down from the second-floor balconies. Others had gathered in the foyer, obviously having stopped on their way to and from the lifts. All clapping madly, whistling, cheering.

Hadley stood guard halfway across the foyer, waving her arms and saying something along the lines of "Nothing to see here."

But then Ted, big, quiet, gentle, gorgeous Ted, slid her down his body till her feet hit the floor, then swept her into a Hollywood dip and kissed her. Thoroughly.

And the crowd went wild.

When he brought her upright, slowly, remembering no doubt that her blood pressure might be a little out of whack considering all the magic and wonder her body was currently in charge of creating, Hadley finally convinced the crowd to: "Get back to work, you vultures, and give them some damn privacy! And if I find out anyone recorded a single frame of that—"

Adelaid didn't hear the rest as Ted caught her attention when he started picking up her bags. Bags she'd let slump the floor.

"May I?" he asked, even as he put them over his shoulder. Showing her that he wasn't going to take her stubbornness lying down. That he still fully intended to call her out, when needed.

"How about we go halves?" she said.

"How about we take turns? This is my turn."

Seriously, she was too tired to argue. It was a nice thing he was doing, and it was nice of her to let him too. So, they came out even.

He held out a hand, waited for her to take it, then led her to his special lift. Once the doors closed, the speed of the thing whipping them skyward.

And Adelaid gasped, "Did I even tell you that I love you?"

He kept watching the floor numbers as if willing them to hurry. "I'm sure you did."

"I don't think so."

His gaze dropped to hers. "Then I must have determined as much, based on evidence. You are, clearly, very much in love with me."

"Very much."

He leaned down, pressed his lips to hers.

She knew love wasn't an easy thing. Wasn't hearts and flowers and chocolate. It was messy and difficult.

Some love came without choice. Her brothers loved her. Her mum had too, in her own volatile way. Her love for her child, while still so fraught and fragile, seemed to grow every second.

Ted *had* a choice. He'd seen her at her messy worst. He'd seen her at her most insecure. He'd seen her when she'd floundered, he'd seen her full of fear. He'd borne the brunt of her distractibility, her jitters, her wobbly relationship with time.

And he loved her anyway.

She'd seen Ted hungry, and grumpy, and all impossibly alpha. She'd also seen him cherish his mother, and support his friends, and work himself to exhaustion to save the world.

And she loved him more.

When the lift doors opened, Ted dumped her bags just outside the door, when there was a perfectly good series of hooks and shelves on which to place such things.

Then he lifted her into his arms and kissed her like a man starved.

Knowing how grateful the man was to eat when he was truly hungry, she laughed against his mouth. Then buckled in for the ride.

EPILOGUE

"I'M OFF!" ADELAID CALLED, quickly checking if Fuzz Lightyear and Spikesaurus Rex needed water, but both looked happy on the windowsill next to one another, arms reaching towards the watery sunlight shining through her new kitchen windows.

For they'd found they needed a place with lots of rooms for Adelaid to work in, and near enough to Big Think for an easy commute. A mini lair for Ted so that he could work from home when needs be, and a library filled with biographies of amazing women and Booker Prize winners and romance novels and dense scientific texts so they could snuggle up and read side by side. A nursery, for their daughter, Katie. That had been important too.

Adelaid licked icing sugar off her fingers and bounced out of the kitchen and down the hall towards the front door, slipping on her "new" second-hand brogues. Although she was making better money now, and she'd landed herself a billionaire, she still loved her vintage gear.

Only to find Ted already there, sunlight streaming through the beautiful, colourful leadlight front door, casting a golden glow over his beastly gorgeousness.

Ted turned, wearing her smudged and rarely used pink glasses, having not been able to locate his own. He held an insulated lunch box in his hand, Katie, their teething five-month-old, on his hip, gnawing on his shoulder and leaving pools of drool on the cotton of his button-down shirt.

"For me?" she asked.

Ted pretended she meant the drooly nibbler, but Adelaid ducked out of the way, before leaning in to kiss her arm cheek. Then snatched the lunch box instead. Adelaid opened it up to find a healthy salad, a banana and a blueberry muffin. Good man.

"Who are you meeting today?" Ted asked, hitching Katie higher on his hip. Then he checked his watch—his father's watch, beautifully refurbished after its fall, its newish face already scratched from when Katie first learned to roll and Ted had reached out to catch her.

"Oh, only the star of the new Lois Lane movie." Adelaid leaned in and rubbed noses with their daughter, before running a hand over her strawberry blond curls. "She's just been diagnosed with Asperger's, and I have the exclusive."

"Smart girl."

She glanced through the leadlight to find her driver had arrived. "How about you? What are your plans today?"

"Saving the world, cleaning rusk out of my hair."

"So, the usual."

"Yep. Sid is coming over to check on the solar panels and Mum will no doubt find an excuse to pop in. Might put on a movie with this one. Thinking five months is old enough now for her first showing of *Calamity Jane*."

Adelaid mock gasped. "Don't you dare! Not without me."

"Fine."

"Now, Muffin, you give Daddy hell, okay? It's your right and your role as a daughter." The Smudge nickname had gone by the wayside the moment they'd seen fingers and toes, all twenty of which Ted still considered a minor miracle.

For a man who'd seriously never considered fatherhood, he was a natural. Just as she'd expected. A beautiful calm balance for Adelaid's wilder ups and downs.

"When she's sixteen, maybe," said Ted, laying a kiss atop his daughter's curls. "Till then, let's aim for Daddy's Little Girl."

"Or?"

"Or she can give me hell. Entirely up to her."

One last kiss for her daughter, another for her

man, Adelaid walked out onto her front porch, several bags looped over her shoulder.

Dressed for the life she wanted, which also happened to be the life she had.

* * * * *

Look out for the second book in the
Billion-Dollar Bachelors trilogy
by Ally Blake
Fake Engagement with the Billionaire
coming in the spring!
And the third book
Cinderella Assistant to Boss's Bride
coming in the fall!

And if you enjoyed this story, check out these
other great reads from Ally Blake

The Wedding Favor
The Millionaire's Melbourne Proposal
Dream Vacation, Surprise Baby

Available now!